About the Author

My journey from sixteen to the recent now, has gone from O-Levels to a spirit level. Many other tools, too, as I became a tradesman. Communication is like food to me, and I've always wanted to write. So, here I am with this completed book. Sometimes, a fear of failure stopped me from doing things. Though somehow not with writing, and I have enjoyed my journey with this book. I hope you enjoy it, too.

A Foreign Plot

Francis Quirke

A Foreign Plot

Vanguard Press

VANGUARD PAPERBACK

© Copyright 2024
Francis Quirke

The right of Francis Quirke to be identified as author of
this work has been asserted by him in accordance with the
Copyright, Designs and Patents Act 1988.

All Rights Reserved

No reproduction, copy or transmission of this publication
may be made without written permission.
No paragraph of this publication may be reproduced,
copied or transmitted save with the written permission of the
publisher, or in accordance with the provisions
of the Copyright Act 1956 (as amended).

Any person who commits any unauthorised act in relation to
this publication may be liable to criminal
prosecution and civil claims for damages.

A CIP catalogue record for this title is
available from the British Library.

ISBN 978 1 83794 083 7

This is a work of fiction. Names, characters, businesses, places, events and
incidents are either the product of the author's imagination or used in a
fictitious manner. Any resemblance to actual persons, living or dead, or actual
events is purely coincidental.

Vanguard Press is an imprint of
Pegasus Elliot Mackenzie Publishers Ltd.
www.pegasuspublishers.com

First Published in 2024

Vanguard Press
Sheraton House Castle Park
Cambridge England

Printed & Bound in Great Britain

To my departed mother and father

Thanks to Eddie, Babs and Janet for having been my test readers. Mustn't forget Elaine and team in Pegasus for giving me this wonderful opportunity to be published. Finally, back to the age of eleven and my English teacher, Mr Hall. He singled me out in class for his only praise for a comprehension we wrote on a novel. His forceful praise that day stayed with me over all the years. It helped me believe I could write.

Chapter 1

There he was – finally! Charlie Funble stepped out of the car and onto the town's central square. He thanked and paid the taxi driver, then watched him drive off. The car disappeared into a narrow, shaded side street, making Charlie feel alone and abandoned. Though, at the same time glad, so he could focus a hundred percent on the task ahead. Turning his head to face the town square, his sense of isolation deepened and weakened him for a moment. He now wished the driver was still present to accompany him. Apart from company, he might have helped him with his quest, for Charlie didn't know how to proceed from the square. Still standing on the same spot, he scanned the view in front of him through squinted eyes. The day was hot, bright, and Charlie was already feeling the prickly heat. He studied the square and saw it dotted with a few elderly locals looking lifeless. He mused at how they looked like old mechanical toys stopped moving. Similar to old metal ones with keys in their backs, needing a wind to get them going.

Having previously looked at countless online pictures of Ovineshta town, he could finally see it looked just like he imagined. It was a quiet, sleepy settlement on the foothills of Bulgaria's Pirin Mountains. His senses were eager to register any strange smells, sights or sounds – this being his first visit. Though at the same time, he felt uncomfortable with the possibility that everyone was secretly watching him. Being a north European of pale complexion, he knew that even a local dog could see he was a stranger. Quickly rationalizing all this, he thought, "How stupid can I be? No one here knows me, so don't be so suspicious." His mindset was such because he felt the town's residents had learnt of his distant dealings with Ovineshta. After all, it was three years previous when he had decided to pick this place for his venture. So, he thought surely everyone must know of his interests with the town by now! It was a foolish notion of his, because he had never spoken with anyone local over the three years. His suspicions were simply a case of paranoia.

From fear of drawing unwanted attention to himself, Charlie thought he'd better make some kind of movement, to show the purpose of his arrival. "Mm, now which exit from the square should I take?" he pondered. Scanning his options allowed him to survey the square and see its attractive layout. Roads exited from each corner with one corner having two, forming a V-shaped exit. Having to use his sense of direction made him feel a little foreboding. It reminded him of a time in London when giving directions to a tourist went horribly wrong. Then to Charlie's amazement, the same tourist approached him an hour later, asking for the same directions. The irate tourist hadn't recognised him on the second encounter. It was raining and

Charlie had since donned a cap and pulled his collar up, partially disguising his face. The tourist complained about having been given wrong directions, unaware he was speaking to the same person.

"Some fool gave me wrong directions an hour ago," he bawled. Charlie was sure his directions were correct and wanted to vindicate himself while remaining incognito. So, he replied, "I noticed you said, he gave you wrong directions and not the wrong directions. Anyway, no matter because, either way, how do you know they were wrong directions? If you've never visited the destination before now, you're not qualified to judge. Some directions appear wrong because they take longer to get you to a destination. His directions might have taken you there had you not given up on them. So, your claim could be subjective thinking." The tourist did well to stay listening to Charlie's bamboozling defence and finally burst out saying, "Are you related to the fool guy, or some kind of nut? I don't get you defending him. I just want to go to…" Charlie stopped the subterfuge and quickly directed him once again, in case of being recognised.

Refocusing back to his present difficulty, the choice of street suddenly became apparent. Rolling his eyes upwards, a clue appeared in front of him. He saw a landmark he recognised from pictures on his computer back in London. The landmark was a good reference point for his destination. It was a small bald patch on top of one of the Pirin's peaks. Its slopes were forested but for a single visible round clearing on the peak. The image was etched on Charlie's mind from first sight of it on his computer, three years previous in 2004. Though, for not nearly as long as the one appearing on the top of his head! Inspired by seeing the helpful landmark, he strode purposefully towards it. He exited the corner of the square with the fork roads, taking the street which looked like the most direct route. His heartbeat sped up with excitement at seeing the bald peak. It was no longer just in his imagination or viewed on a computer screen. It was there, for real, and right in front of him. Like a friendly finger coaxing him towards it.

It was one o'clock and the day very hot. Particularly hot for a March, with a stinging heat from high humidity. Though, any feeling of discomfort was more than offset by wondrous thoughts of discovery. The street he took from the square had an incline and surfaced with well-worn tarmac. A few old and ornate pre-communist buildings stood either side of the street. They were badly neglected, but still beautiful enough to attract attention from anyone passing. Charlie wondered at the stories these decadent buildings could tell. He thought how out of place they looked in this poor farming town. Olive trees lined the street, their leaves rustling in a gentle breeze coming off the mountains. All these new sights and sounds were a pleasant distraction from the walk, because he became uncomfortable from the heat. His trousers were snagging on his knees from sweat. While momentarily looking down at his mild discomfort, a cock suddenly flew across his head. It gave him an awful fright! Being caught unawares instinctively made him raise his hands up and cower for cover. His reaction was understandable, as he had never experienced anything that big flying across his face before.

Though he did momentarily recall something smaller which had crossed his face. It was a slap from a woman's hand. It happened one night during his more youthful days in a busy bar. He was having a lively and stimulating chat with a woman. Charlie had only met her for the first time that night and there was an instant attraction between them. This led into feeling the need to impress the other. So, their conversation flowed effortlessly and covered all sorts of topics. They talked about human characteristics and emotions, such as embarrassment, pain, recklessness, risk taking, reward, etcetera. He told the woman there was nothing that could embarrass him. She told him her claim was never having been wrong about anything. She offered to prove he was wrong about his claim and in doing so, proving her own claim. Charlie said, "Okay prove your point now."

She suddenly slapped his face and waited for a few seconds and said, "See, I'm right. You're blushing and embarrassed." She was right because it was the last thing he expected, and the bar was full of people staring! Despite her hostile method in proving him wrong, the woman didn't slap him hard. The few who heard but didn't see the incident jokingly requested a replay. Charlie felt mild consolation knowing that it was the action and not the severity of the slap which caused the embarrassment.

Standing straight and recomposing himself, Charlie made a sheepish look around to see if anyone saw his fright from the cock. Unfortunately for him, someone did see it. It was noticed by an elderly woman looking straight at him. She was sitting on a bench against a stone wall with a window above. Dressed in black, knees splayed two feet apart, stretching a long ankle-length skirt. He studied her while she fixed him with a long look through a 'stiff' eye. He didn't know whether to acknowledge the woman by nodding or maybe smiling. Before deciding what to do he had already walked past her. He wondered, had she been with someone, would they have laughed at his predicament. "Huh, probably," he thought. The street was narrowing, and its glorious opulent and decadent buildings were behind him. As he progressed upwards, simple stone and brick houses lined the street. Also, its tarmac surface changed to one of firm clay and gravel. Again, it was decision time for Charlie. There was a three-way split in the street ahead and he knew he was coming to the perimeter of the town. Once again, he relied on intuition to help decide which way to go. Looking up at the bald-headed peak also helped. He could see how closer it appeared. This gave him a rush of blood from anticipation of what he was soon to find. His confidence grew with every footstep. It made any possible wrong turning an insignificant delay. For he knew he was close enough to afford himself a directional mistake or two. Time was on his side. There was no hurry. However, he did try to gauge the position of the peak in relation to where he wanted to arrive. He was fully convinced he was about to take the correct approach to his destination. "I think I'll take this one going slightly to the right," he said. The partly gravelled street had become even narrower and more of a dirt lane. He knew he was approaching the very top edge of the town.

Barns replaced the sight of houses on both sides of the lane he walked. From within one, noise of light machinery punctured the quietness of the countryside. He thought he much preferred the sound of insects, gentle wind and rustling leaves, to that of a chainsaw cutting wood. His urgency increased and his pace quickened, stumbling on a stone as he progressed. Sensing he was ever closer to his goal, he totally focused his mind for what he hoped to see. Pessimism set in to tame his bubbling optimism and he told himself, "What if it's not there? What if I've got this all wrong?" Quickly he rationalised that all would be revealed and very tangible at the end of the lane. Then suddenly to his left and without warning, a barn door burst open. Out walked a man holding a chainsaw. Charlie didn't flinch – to his own surprise – and looked at the man. It was the first time he had seen a man up close in the town since he arrived. The moment felt like a scene from a 'Spaghetti Western' because the two locked eyes on each other. The look was long enough for it to count as a stare. Charlie was sweating; he wasn't. The man was well built, had strong, black, uncombed hair, dark olive skin and one long black eyebrow crossing both eyes. It was the eyebrow that captured Charlie's attention, as it reminded him of a rhyme his father once told him. He mentally recited it, 'Beware of the man whose eyebrows meet, for within his eyes there is deceit.' At that same time, he was aware that he must've had his own musings on him. Wondering what they'd be, Charlie jokingly thought, "One of England's finest, I hope."

As earlier with the cock and elderly woman, he carried on walking. His mind was back on the hunt and every step was taking him closer. Each one likened to a layer of wrapping paper taken off a present to finally reveal it! He even started a countdown from fifty, as he was so close to the end of the lane and his prize. "Fifty, forty-nine, forty-eight, forty-seven…" he counted. Then at his count of 'Twelve', Charlie passed the last building and turned his head ninety degrees. The full unobstructed view of the majestic Pirin Mountains appeared. Standing still for a moment, he took in the enormity of the mountain range. He imagined the experience similar to being inside a theatre, where an actor steps into full view of the audience. Meaning, the last barn of the lane represented the side curtain, and the mountains were the audience. With eyes and mouth wide open in delight from the unobstructed view, he said, "Search over." Charlie lowered his eyes to the ground and stared at his goal – his plot of land!

Or did he? Charlie's spontaneous joy was a little premature. He had yet more searching to do, for his plot was among a few. He had yet to locate its exact position. After returning his mood to a more appropriate happy anticipation, he refocused. Remembering another helpful landmark to locate it, he moved further forward through long grass to find it. He thought there should be a junction he recognised from online pictures. It was a barely recognisable T-junction, made up of two dirt roads with no road signs to highlight it. The only defining characteristic was the beige-brown colour of the roads, carving their way through green grass. He was carving his own trail through the grass as he walked. Charlie felt he was in the second act of a play. He looked up and was convinced he could see a grin appear on the mountain face. "Yes, it knows I'm very close to actually standing on my piece of Bulgaria," he said. Again, moving further forward, he could at last make out the shape of the junction. Then, a few moments later, he felt the gentle lash of long grass against his ankles ease. For he was about to step onto the edge of one of those dirt roads. Right across the road was his plot! He knew this instantly, because his plot's boundary formed one of the 'T' junction's two corners. Also, he knew which corner from having studied the online pictures back in London. Crossing over to stand on its boundary, Charlie stood still and finally looked at his parcel of land.

The quest was now over. He welled up with pride from his achievement. His mind drifted into a dreamscape. One in which townsfolk came out of their houses smiling, cheering and lining the dirt road to his plot. He is walking between them, looking at outstretched arms and listening to clapping in praise of him! Having wallowed for a while in his self–congratulation, he strolled onto his land. There were no boundary markings, but he knew the size and approximate perimeter locations. Walking around it like a farmer examining land, he took notice of every piece of growth and divot. Then standing still again, inhaling deeply and looking upwards, the air seemed sweeter and its view more wondrous. It was while doing this that he had a change of mind regarding his wish for anonymity. Now, he wished someone would come out and say 'hello' and probe him about his presence, so he could proudly talk about his land. Then, walking out of the plot, he turned around to stare at its entirety. He dreamt of a fine traditional Bulgarian house standing on it one day.

It was always a dream of Charlie to build a house since a teenager. What to do with it afterwards only required consideration as he got older and a possible change in lifestyle. Despite the years passing there was time to plan and decide, though he still didn't have an answer. He hoped one would eventually come to him.

Its location was perfect, being on the upper edge of the town boundary with a couple other adjoining plots. Some properties were near enough to give his land a sense of belonging, while at the same time, keeping an appearance of openness without looking isolated. Though, above all, he knew its best quality was its closeness to the foothills of the Pirin Mountains. It had a fantastic unobstructed view of them. The Rila and Rhodope Mountain ranges were also visible to the left and right of his plot. They all formed a horseshoe around it and Charlie hoped a lucky horseshoe too! Turning to look at the bald headed peak once more, he said quietly, "Thanks for the help."

He strolled away from his plot feeling a success. Until that point, his mind had been consumed with just one thought – finding the plot. It was clear now, free to pick and choose anything he wanted to do. He decided to do something simple, unchallenging and rewarding, like having a beer, or maybe buying something. It wasn't long before he saw a car parked with three men inside. He thought, "I'll ask the driver if there's a taxi in the town." His decision to approach the car was to lead Charlie into an episode of terror.

The driver, on hearing Charlie say the word 'taxi', smiled and gestured for him to get into the car. Charlie surmised that people in an undeveloped town like Ovineshta improvised to make a wage. Meaning, farmers with land and a car acted as part-time taxi drivers to make extra money. So, into the car he climbed, door closed and off it went. The following scene didn't amount to a huge length of time. Though it created a period of confusion extremely tense enough to make Charlie curse his being there.

The driver and two other men started talking as they drove off. As the car headed upwards towards the top edge of the town, the driver kept turning around and talking Bulgarian to him in an assertive way. Charlie didn't know if his tone was angry or just the way he normally spoke. No matter, it perplexed him enough to become anxious. His eyes were peeled to see if the driver would make his way round to the main road for Bonkas. The car took a left which made sense but then turned right - which didn't! "Mm don't panic yet, he may be taking another route," thought Charlie. Regardless, Charlie decided to say, "Bonkas, Bonkas," to show urgency and seriousness of his request.

Over the next few moments, he realised the car was not heading for the town exit. His heartbeat rose and anxiety heightened with every second. The car was going deeper into the town, while visions of the man with the chainsaw came to his mind. To make matters worse, the man sitting next to him was smiling and making the occasional laugh. The other two in front talked and made quizzical looks at Charlie. "Oh my God, these people are either numb skulls or psycho killer kidnappers!" thought Charlie. The fear and chaos building in his mind was akin to the sudden chaos in a household hearing of a surprise visit. The normal order was no longer in place. The same was happening to Charlie's mind but with the added element of fear. His chaotic mind created a strange train of thoughts. It started with the word 'kidnapped', and Charlie suddenly pondered how strange a word it was to describe a person taken against their will. It could almost appear to mean a young goat (kid) being taken against its will, or a young child. That lead him to suddenly think of the word 'catnapping'. To someone with poor understanding of English, it could mean a cat taken against its will. These thoughts might have amused and weighed longer on his mind at another time. Though, right now, he was more interested in why the car was not going to Bonkas.

"Stop... let me out, I want to go to Bonkas, let me out," he shouted. It was as though he wasn't there because the three men only talked among themselves, ignoring his plea. Adding to the suspense was the man next to Charlie. He made the occasional laugh accompanied by a sideways sneer. Hitchcock films next appeared in Charlie's mind! The car was driving farther and farther away from the town's exit. It bounced along on the dirt roads, into and out of some potholes. Its tyres flicked small stones with their edges as they drove over them. Then suddenly... the car stopped abruptly! Charlie knew this was his chance to escape.

Out of the car he jumped and started to walk briskly up the stony lane. Strangely enough, he decided to walk and not run. He quickly made that choice to avoid showing too much fear and therefore weakness. It might anger the men should they decide to chase and capture him. So, he thought if he escaped using just a brisk walk, it would show a more contained character and less fear. A kind of masculine fear – if such a thing existed! Also, his action might gain more respect and therefore leniency should they be violent and decide on punishing him. Things worsened and fear increased because the man sitting next to him came out of the car and ran after him! Charlie never turned to look but could hear his shoes on the gravel. He quickly formed a plan of action for when he got close. He would punch him in the face or knee him in the groin giving him numb 'nuts' to go with his numb skull! Charlie knew the car had to drive in reverse to catch up with him. That would allow Charlie more time to escape, than if the car was front facing. However, that didn't happen.

When the man reached Charlie, he grinned in a likeable way. While taking his arm with one hand, he pointed back at the car with the other. Those three unexpected actions happened simultaneously, not allowing Charlie any time to decide a reaction. That momentary indecision made him involuntarily look up at the direction of the man's finger. He saw a woman bending down talking with the driver. "Right... this may not be as serious as I'm thinking," he thought. The appearance of the woman settled Charlie's mind and he tentatively walked back to the car with the man.

On returning to the car, the woman looked up, smiled and said, "Hello, I'm Emily, a schoolteacher, and I speak English. These men asked me to translate your English. They are curious about your visit here and want to ask about you. They have been driving around the town trying to find someone who speaks English." Charlie gave a huge sigh of relief, and everyone laughed after hearing the reason for his confusion, anxiety and sudden exit from the car. After everyone spoke and the helpful woman left, Charlie said goodbye to the men. They hadn't forgotten he was destined for Bonkas and reinforced their original offer of the lift. Notwithstanding, Charlie politely declined as was in the mood for a spell of quiet solitude, to re-run events just passed. He walked to the town square in the hope of finding a taxi, but…! It was a second ordeal which awaited him!

Chapter 2

On arriving in the square, he asked a man where he could find a taxi. His request was received with a shrug of his shoulders. Charlie moved on to the only other person nearby, an elderly man in a thick jacket. He admired him for being able to wear any jacket on the hot humid day. So much so, he decided not to be disappointed should he not be able to help. The man raised an arm and pointed at a hotel across the town square. Crossing the square, Charlie anticipated no one in the hotel spoke English too. He walked up the steps of the old sixties-style building to enquire. It took him five to seven minutes before he found a staff member. She was a young girl who could speak some English and was keen to use what she knew. Unfortunately for her, the remoteness of the town didn't attract enough English-speaking tourists with which to practise. Unfortunate too, was her telling him no taxi office existed in Ovineshta. He sighed, thanked her, left and walked down the steps to ponder his next move. Standing still, he squeezed his lip with two fingers, as though it would help him find a solution. He made a casual look across the square and was intrigued to see a crowd had gathered. One of the two people from whom he made enquiries was at its centre. All were looking straight across the square at him. Someone in the middle of the crowd was holding up a sheet of paper at arm's length for others to read. Another was pointing a finger in Charlie's direction.

"Mm, what's that about? Why are they looking at me and one pointing? Maybe it's not me, maybe he's pointing at the hotel or the mountain. Or maybe it's some big latest news on that sheet of paper. Yes, I bet that's it, livestock prices, or the price of nuts have gone up. They like eating a lot of nuts here," he mumbled. He looked away and didn't spend any longer attempting to understand the gathering. Still thinking about a lift to Bonkas, he exited the square by the corner furthest from the crowd. He was only a short distance down the lane when a darting shadow crossed the road in front of him.

Then, for no reason but for an involuntary action, he took a quick look over his shoulder. Expecting to see an isolated corner, he was shocked to see the crowd had followed him. "Must be intuition that made me look," he thought. All the crowd stood motionless and stared at Charlie. As with any unusual or unexplained sight, it was a little unnerving. Initial curiosity now turned to anxiety for the second time in Charlie that day. He suddenly decided to change his priorities to dealing with the crowd.

The individuals were dressed in black and looked like locals of mixed ages. All were expressionless and two men were holding a billhook and machete. Their image both confused and worried Charlie. It was because, despite looking like a lynch mob, they didn't show the aggression of one. The sight of the two cutting implements made his eyes widen and eyebrows rise, causing sweat to run into them. They stung and Charlie worried the sweat made him look as though he was crying. He hoped the men with the tools were returning from work in the fields, only casually joining the crowd. That, rather than them purposely taking the tools to become weapons!

"Yes, that's it, they're just returning from work and besides, they'll be too knackered to chase me if they decide to do so. I'll be able to outrun them," he thought. The staring continued and more sweat ran into his eyes, making him see twice as many people from the sweat's refraction. He wiped his eyes clear and – thankfully – the crowd reduced in size to reappeared as its original number. Deciding to turn and walk away, he eventually jogged to the square via another route. Being out in the open square rather than in the quiet lanes of the town was a safer option. "God, what's going wrong today? I'm not yet a day in Bulgaria and already there's a lynch mob after me," he said as he jogged.

Reaching the square and not wanting to waste time, he quickly scanned its perimeter for any official-looking building for a refuge. There was one which came into view with a big crest above its door and looked official. Charlie headed for the entrance and went inside. Not before time too, as the crowd weren't far behind him and soon arrived outside. It became larger and rowdier, now resembling a mob. While feeling the safety of being inside and peering out at it, he heard the gentle voice of a woman speaking.

She said in clear English, "Can I help you sir?" He turned around to see a good-looking, well-dressed woman with an attentive manner. Unbeknownst to Charlie, she was the town mayoress.

"Hello and nice to meet you. Sorry but I wonder can you tell me why half your town is chasing after me? I'm not yet one day in your country and I seem to have become very unpopular," he said.

"Have you done anything to cause such a reaction?" she asked.

"No, nothing." Replied Charlie.

"I'm ever so sorry, let me go out and talk with them," said the mayoress. He watched her approach the crowd and the man with the sheet of paper held it open in front of her. A lively conversation took place of which Charlie could only guess its content. The mayoress looked up at him while Charlie stared back out of the window. She pointed and smiled, followed by the mob suddenly smiling and eventually laughing! With the threat seemingly dispelled, his anxiety turned to annoyance at being ridiculed in the play unfolding. The mob returned to a crowd again for a moment before disbursing. The mayoress climbed back up the steps to Charlie still waiting inside.

She smiled again and said, "Okay, let me explain. Firstly, what is your name, please?"

"Charlie, Charlie Funble," he replied.

"Mr Fumball, do not be afraid, and it's all a misunderstanding. One of the villagers saw your image on a police poster," she stated.

"Police poster!" exclaimed Charlie.

"Yes, a taxi car was stolen earlier today, and the police were given a mobile phone picture of you standing by the cab appearing as the driver. So, you were the culprit until the real thief was caught. The police said they caught the real car thief on his way to the Greek border. He left the stolen taxi on the highway to walk the rest of the way, after running out of petrol," said the mayoress.

"But why was I connected?" Charlie replied with a confused look.

"The thief had a picture of you on his phone which he gave to a nearby police station. Police immediately produced posters and circulated them in nearby settlements. A resident here saw it sometime today and realised you were the man in the poster. That's why they followed you," replied the mayoress.

"Ah, I see, and I can explain how he had my picture. He suggested taking a couple holiday pictures of me standing by the car. He must have switched phones to use his own for the second snap. That was so he could frame me for stealing the car. He must've gone into a police station and reported me as the thief, showing that picture he took of me as proof," said Charlie.

"Yes probably, and the car thief finally revealed his guilt to a patrol car. The patrol car officer saw him walking south towards the Greek border. The empty parked taxi with driver's door open was seen parked a short distance from him," she replied.

"Phew, thank God that's solved. Amazing to think he had the gall to take lifts too – after stealing the taxi," exclaimed Charlie.

"What! Was there a girl involved too?" asked the mayoress

"Ha no, I said 'gall' not 'girl'. Gall means cheeky," he replied.

They both turned to look out of the window for a well needed pause in their discussion. After fifteen seconds or so and while both were looking outside, Charlie said, "You won't believe the other scary incident I had here today. I think I'll change my name to 'Stumble' as I've been stumbling from one mishap to the next."

The mayoress didn't understand and enquired, "Sorry?"

To which Charlie said, "Oh don't worry. I must say, your English is great, but just for my name, it's Funble – not Fumball. Sorry, I've been rude not asking yours. What is it, please?"

The mayoress smiled and replied, "Evdokiya and you're allowed to mispronounce it many times, as it's not easy to remember. I'll give you a lift back to your hotel because of your trouble today." He assured her all was fine, that he held no bad feelings and hoped to see he again.

After getting out of Mayoress Evdokiya's car in Bonkas and saying goodbye, he stood still and thought about what to do. He didn't want to go back to his room straight away, as the late afternoon was still gorgeous, hot and sunny. Spotting a nearby *mehana*, it reminded Charlie he'd been keen on trying his first Bulgarian beer since arriving. Right now, it seemed especially appropriate, too, to celebrate finding his plot. Though before walking over to the entrance, he looked around the nearby area. He wanted to see if there was anything that could persuade him to stay out in the sun and stop him from going inside. The colours of a fruit and vegetable market caught his eye, particularly the bananas. Their bright yellow colour seemed to stand out from all the other fruit, in the same way as the bald mountain peak stood out from the other peaks in Ovineshta.

He hadn't eaten since breakfast, so he strolled over to buy two of them to eat straight away. The calm nature of the stall owners was a lure for Charlie too. They weren't frantic and combative in selling their produce like many in London. He supposed there was no need, as rural Bulgarian markets were fewer and had bigger catchments of people compared to those in London.

"Mm, lovely, I've never tasted bananas so sweet," he enthused. The sweet after taste in his mouth was stronger than he'd ever tasted from bananas before, so he decided to stand and savour it for a while. Enjoying the taste so much was gradually putting him off trying that beer, which would cancel the taste. With that conflict of decision, he decided to delegate his decision to temptation. He gave it full responsibility with making up his mind. Obviously for temptation to be able to work, Charlie had to move closer to the *mehana*. So, he strolled over to the entrance, but still didn't feel any lure to go in. "Mm still don't know if I want to go in," he thought. The banana was winning. Then, just as he edged closer to the door, a man came out. A waft of beer immediately followed him before the door closed. It brushed Charlie's nostrils. The smell of that beer immediately mitigated the taste of the bananas. He thought a battle of senses had taken place and olfactory had won. He had a quick look through a window at the side of the door, then went in.

Mehanas are Bulgarian rustic restaurants with lovely country character. They have stone walls from which farming tools hang, and on the floors stand strong dark wooden benches, chairs and tables. Embroidered tablecloths lie across their tops. Often a clay and brick oven is in one corner. Floors are stone and give that aura of old-world charm.

Charlie sat down and faced another huge decision in the day – what to drink! Was it to be a pint of Zagorka or Pirinsko? He decided to have the Pirinsko as it was particular to the area and eagerly waited for its arrival onto his table. "Here it comes," he said, treating the whole experience as an informal ceremony. He was looking forward to his first taste so much that he hardly took notice of the lovely waitress bringing it to him. "*Mersi*," said Charlie with eyes fixed on the glass, then he took his first mouthful of Bulgarian beer. He took another before passing judgement because the first mouthful had to wash away the taste of banana. "Arrr, lovely," he said quietly.

Sitting back on his bench, he reflected on his day so far. He thought about events in Ovineshta. He decided to play with creating a headline for the day while he drank his beer. He smiled as one came to him… "Man Finds Plot, Only to Lose Plot, Over Mistaken Kidnap Plot!" Charlie brought his empty glass back to the counter, thanked the staff and left for his hotel.

After a comfortable night's sleep, he woke to a new day. The first sound he heard was that of small animals in the back gardens of houses nearby. It reminded him of the cock which flew past his face the previous day. On reflection, he thought he was lucky it didn't land on his head. They couldn't fly too far or high so his head could have become a handy perch for a moment's rest. He packed his luggage after one more night's sleep to leave Bulgaria. The hotel was nicely located on the main road going up through Bonkas. It had a big glass window on its corner, allowing guests a wonderful view of Mount Vihren beyond the top of town. His flight was from the Sofia International Airport in the late afternoon, and he decided to take a coach to the capital. His Bulgarian visit was only three days, but he was happy with that length of stay. It was a 'search and find' one rather than a proper holiday. The Sofia coach's route passed villages and towns on the N19 road – Ovineshta being one of them. With some spare time, Charlie decided to take a taxi from his hotel to Ovineshta for one last look. His plot now located allowed him to wander and dream of plans for his land. Then, he could stroll down through the town and cross the main road to the coach stop on the other side.

He arrived at the stop with thirty minutes to spare. Parking his suitcase and bag to one side, he turned around to face the town he had just left. His head was up, and eyes closed, facing the hot sun. Occasionally he opened them to look at the bald mountain peak way off in the distance. The coach stop had a 1960s concrete and glass building which served as a ticket office and snack shop. The day had a lovely dry heat, unlike the previous more humid one. He decided to stay standing outside to enjoy it for a while.

"Ah, what a successful trip, mm, I think I'll go inside and check confirmation of the bus time." he said. Still filled with pride from the success of his previous day's quest, he felt invincible as he walked across the polished marble floor. Looking like a man called to receive an award, with chest expanded and head held high, he stopped at the ticket kiosk. He had to bend down considerably to talk to counter staff through a small service hatch. This was a commonplace design feature from Bulgaria's past and made enquiries difficult for tall people. It was a product of the old regime with a society having no sense of 'customer service'. So, authorities thought, it was sufficient for kiosks to have small hip-height openings for hand-to-hand transactions.

Sticking his head halfway through the opening to be clearly heard, Charlie spoke to the woman. She looked threatened by his overly friendly approach and didn't like the invasion of her space. "Hello, excuse me, can you tell me when the next bus for Sofia arrives, please?" he said. Halfway into the question, he knew he wasn't going to get a speedy answer – if any at all. He could see that the woman was middle aged and most likely local. It meant a strong possibility she couldn't speak English. Also, her having to deal with an English-speaking head protruding through her service hatch didn't promise much for Charlie. Her face had an irate expression and she remained silent. He had no clue whatsoever to the response he would receive.

After a pause, he repeated the question to which she fired a terse reply in Bulgarian. Sensing possible tension developing from a further repeat of the question, Charlie attempted to rephrase it. It made matters worse. She frantically waved an arm, shouted something in Bulgarian and attempted to close the hatch on Charlie's head.

"Maybe she saw that police poster," he thought. Despite feeling a little deflated, Charlie still retained his pride. He hadn't lost it all from that awkward episode. Otherwise, he would have felt like an empty sack, unable to walk away. To restore his confidence, he decided to pick a simpler challenge.

Spotting a snack shop, he walked over to it with steely determination to buy a bottle of water. He knew this was achievable so long as he didn't have to speak. All he had to do was point at the water, like a monkey at a banana. Then, offer a note with a big enough denomination of leva. That would avoid any complicated conversation about giving the correct amount. It worked! However, as he turned to walk away, he was sure the shop assistant cursed him for taking all his change!

The coach arrived on time at twelve noon, and he climbed aboard. Remembering how hot the coach had become on his journey down from Sofia, he pondered over which side to sit. He wanted to be comfortable this time, as a three-hour journey in hot weather on a coach with no air conditioning wasn't pleasant. To be honest, calling it a coach was a bit of an overstatement because it was more a minibus. Leg room was very minimal, seats were narrow, and a passenger's comfort depended a lot on who was sitting next to them. Parts of the journey were very bumpy and with sudden jolts. Handrails in front of the seats had to be grabbed often and suddenly to steady oneself. Then, if the passenger next to them was a beefy farmer with big hands and a bad aim, their journey had perilous moments. Should he and a beefy farmer have to suddenly grab the rail in front, a cherished little finger could be in potential danger. It could be reduced to resemble a smear of putty, should it end up between the rail and 'Mr Beefy's' hand..

Charlie, realising this early into his journey, dreamt of someone facing the same problem and deciding to grab the rail with their teeth instead of their hand. Then unfortunately, the opposite happened. The finger of the beefy farmer was nearly bitten off from a bad aim by the other's mouth grab. Despite not taking his thoughts seriously, he knew they occupied his mind for some of the journey time. There was the loud shaking, rattling of fixtures and fittings adding to discomfort. The stop at Blagoevgrad was the only one before Sofia. Passengers disembarked and others boarded. It was obviously better that more passengers got off than on. It made the remaining journey more pleasant because of more room becoming available. It was three o'clock when he arrived at Sofia's city outskirts on a half-full minibus.

The only curiosity on the journey had been an elderly woman passenger and her phone. Every so often, someone would ring her, and it would activate a loud, aggressive rap song ringtone. It provided regular amusement for Charlie because he couldn't get a funnier contrasting sight. That of an elderly, toothless rural woman, with a rap song for her phone's ringtone! He compared the funny distraction to when he was a child going on long car journeys. Every so often he would turn around to look at the nodding head of a toy dog on the back shelf of his parents' car. On later reflection, Charlie assumed the old woman was given the phone by a member of her family. A lot of Bulgaria's younger, more educated and adaptable workforce were moving to the capital for work. The country was transitioning from an antiquated past to a more modern one. This meant that a lot of parents still living in the towns and villages had to travel to Sofia to see sons and daughters. The contrast created by a Bulgaria in transition coincided with Charlie's own contrast within. That being a contrast of thoughts. Did he want to remain living in a metropolis, or move to a less congested environment – like a countryside? Did he want to remain single, or join and commit to a woman? He hoped the answers to those questions would eventually appear. He knew there could be other motives for building a house far from home, other than to satisfy a practical challenge. If there was another reason or reasons, it or they were deep in his conscience, yet to surface.

The minibus finally arrived at Ovcha Kupel coach terminal in Sofia. Its location in the west side made it difficult for passengers wanting to go onto the airport the same day, as Sofia International was in the east side. Charlie disembarked, collected his suitcase and bag, then looked across the compound for an 'OK Taxi' driver. He had read on a Bulgarian tourist guide that 'OK Taxi' was recommended as being bona fide. Many unscrupulous taxi companies and drivers were operating on the roads, making choosing one perilous. At Ovcha Kupel, there was no taxi rank where everyone formed an orderly queue. The coach station's arrangement was for arriving passengers to choose from a random selection of taxis. Charlie strolled – rather than walking quickly – towards the taxis, so he could take time to choose his driver. They were clearly visible, as all of them were standing by their cars enjoying the sun. The airport journey was an hour's drive, so he wanted as pleasurable a journey as possible. The drivers fixed him with stares, as if they had magnetic eyes to pull him towards their cars for the trade. "Mm, I think that one will do, yes, he looks a warm, affable fellow," he thought. Both men greeted each other while not understanding a word either spoke. Charlie, wearing a playful smile and thinking of the stolen taxi saga, pointed to the vehicle and smiled asking, "Stolen? Yes, no?" He held his arms outstretched at his sides to signify a plane for a flight and said, "Five pm," while pointing to his watch.

The driver eagerly agreed and said, "Da." Both got into the car, delighted with the smooth physical communication being understood by both. However, an unbeknownst Charlie didn't realise the driver was heading for a church and not the airport. The driver had mistaken his outstretched arms for Jesus on a cross!

Sofia's roads were infamous for having traffic jams and lack of parking spaces. The road network was a mix of narrow one-way streets and much wider boulevards acting as road arteries. There was a new ring road in progress, and it was causing huge disruption for traffic on the outer routes. This became very real for him and the driver being only ten minutes into the journey, because the traffic slowed and eventually stopped. Charlie was very concerned because of the fear of missing his flight. The driver was also rightly concerned, but for the wrong reason. He thought his passenger would miss Mass! Both fretted and looked at their watches as the traffic moved again. The driver pointed to the radio/cassette on the dashboard, childishly looking at Charlie for approval to switch it on.

He nodded and said, "Yes, of course. It's your car after all." He soon realized that his act of compliance with the driver's wish would be a big regret. He gleefully switched on the radio/cassette and immediately out poured a sexually charged rap song. Turning up the volume to near full, the driver roared out in unison with the song's lyrics,

"I got big power between my legs, but yooz control it, ya know ya want to and like it babyyyy!" Charlie fixed the driver with a stare of anguish and disbelief. The driver's face was contorted and mimicked an expression of someone trying to pass a stubborn 'stool'. His eyes weren't just closed, but squeezed tightly closed, while his tongue stuck out of his mouth while shouting the 'yyyy' of 'babyyyy'.

The tongue part of the performance puzzled Charlie as he thought it impossible for anyone to say 'baby' with their tongue sticking out of their mouth. He even tried it himself, while pushing his head back against the headrest so the driver wouldn't see. He was unsuccessful. He convinced himself the ability being dependant on the mouth anatomy of those speaking certain languages. Baseball hat back to front and nodding to the barely recognisable music, the driver was lost to all around him. He continued nodding his head, eagerly awaiting the next 'I got big power…' lyric. Charlie concluded that people not speaking English wouldn't be able to judge the approval rating of certain English words. So, hearing any controversial words in a song wouldn't register with them. They'd happily sing along, ignorant to any meaning. He hoped the traffic would get moving again in case his driver decided to engage in any other activities to annoy him! The song ended and the traffic moved a little faster. Thankfully for Charlie, the driver returned to normality, as though being released from a nasty curse.

After another ten minutes, the driver turned to Charlie, smiled and pointed ahead. Charlie frowned and was obviously confused because the only thing he saw was a looming church spire! He decided to fear the worst, which was the driver taking him to the church. He guessed correct and waited until the car stopped twenty feet from its door for confirmation. Not a church confirmation, of course, but a confirmation of being taken to a church – instead of an airport. They both sat in silence for three seconds. Charlie stared at the church while the driver stared at Charlie, feeling satisfied with another happy customer.

Then, Charlie lost his temper and exclaimed, "You bloody idiot, I said airport, not a church". Quickly calming he said, "Well, I didn't say airport," then raising his voice again said, "but I did show you a plane, for God's sake! I'm going to miss my plane now". His frustration crescendoed again and he said, "Tch, for God's sake, my arms outstretched meant a plane, not a cross. Why would I be going to a church with luggage, you moron?"

The driver looked very confused, and Charlie sprang out of the car to help him understand. He jumped and ran around the church yard with arms outstretched, pretending to be a plane. Finally, the driver shook his head sideways showing he understood. Then re-establishing his big smile, he beckoned Charlie back into his car. Charlie stared back at him through the windscreen and nearly erupted again, thinking he still didn't recognise his plane impersonation. That was until he quickly remembered a sideways head shake in Bulgaria means 'yes' and a nod was 'no'.

They finally arrived at the airport just on time. Charlie thanked and generously tipped the driver, by way of apology for having been angry with him. He made his way to check-in, passing the translation signs explaining 'Thank you = *Mersi'* and 'Goodbye = *Ciao'* which reminded him how peculiar they seemed at first sight on his arrival. The use of those French and Italian words for day-to-day pleasantries in Bulgaria intrigued him. It was enough to encourage him to make enquiries during his stay. To his surprise, he didn't receive a definitive answer to the curiosity but only a suggestion. He was told they became mainstream words in Bulgaria because of the frequency of Italian and French foreign language films during Communist times. He heard those were the only films allowed for screening during those years. Returning his gaze back to the check-in desk, his present concern was avoiding any unwanted attention to his oversized hand baggage. He hoped his shiny, new leather-bound passport holder would warrant him a prompt sending to departures. It did and he was finally sitting on the plane ready for take-off.

The flight was two and half hours and the first for many Bulgarians on board. They were understandably excited as international travel was becoming more commonplace in the modernising country. It was easy to distinguish those passengers for whom flying was a new phenomenon Some of a mature age behaved giddier than their children. Many hadn't been on anything bigger or higher off the ground than a bus or coach. So, aeroplane passenger protocol was unknown to them. They'd stand in the aisles talking to seated friends and family, as though they were on a bus in Sofia. It was very much to the irritation of the eternally patient hostesses.

Charlie's attention was taken by one giddy man who was standing in the aisle. He'd switch between talking with a seated aisle passenger and craning his neck – like a giraffe – to peer out of a window. This routine of back and forth went on for some time and quickened with his increasing giddiness. Finally forgetting his whereabouts, he leant across two seated passengers to try open a window, forgetting he was thirty-five-thousand feet up in the air!

On landing, applause and cheers were given to the plane's safe arrival because flying was so new to many. Charlie thought it very endearing. While waiting to disembark, he reflected for a moment on his first trip to Bulgaria. He thought mainstream Bulgarians to be an 'earthy' nice people who hadn't been tainted – like many in the world – of the new religion of materialism and wealth. Or, the new 'breed of greed', which Charlie liked to call many wealth chasers of today. Seeing their appreciation of more mundane things prompted him to remind himself to re-evaluate his own list of priorities. He looked forward to more trips.

After 'running the gauntlet' of his journey home from busy Gatwick, he finally arrived at his house. Both feelings of reluctance and melancholy came over him as he approached his front door. The sight of it brought the mundane parts of London life to mind. While taking out his door key, he guessed how much mail was on the doormat. Then, opening the door he took the first smell of home in days. While realizing how a short absence could make him unfamiliar with the smell of his own home, he set down his suitcase and bag in the hall. He picked up the mail and sat down in the kitchen.

Looking up at the clock, he saw it was eleven pm and decided to turn off the table lamp's timer switch. Deciding to go to bed, he next realised his tiredness was a sort which wouldn't let him sleep. It was more a physical tiredness, rather than a mental one. So, he stayed up for a while longer and thought about Ovineshta. At the same time, purposely shutting out thoughts of work trying to barge its way into focus. His further reflections kept memories alive and didn't allow them the slightest chance to fade. Eleven pm became one a.m. and Charlie finally went to bed to dream of further trips to Bulgaria.

Chapter 3

"Ah, hello Mr. Grumble, please wait in reception," said the receptionist at BG Living.

"Err sorry, it's Funble, actually, my name is Mr. Funble," said Charlie while smiling. He thought about saying he was Mr. Grumble only from time to time in deepest, miserable winter. However, he didn't and thought it best to show a more serious manner. He was in the office of BG Living, having decided to research the requirements and costs of building a house on his plot. While searching, he came across BG Living and decided to pay the company a visit. It was a nondescript office in north London, but the few Bulgarian staff gave the drab place an aura of Bulgaria. The ambience immediately heightened pleasant thoughts of his recent trip. It increased his keenness to build a house with every passing minute.

Eventually, he was ushered into a room to meet the company's owner. Her name was Yana. She was a small woman, almost small enough to fit into a drawer of her huge desk. She had long angular eyes, at times giving both sensual and predator looks, half hooded from over generous eyelids. When in a serious mood, they gave her the look of a jaguar ready to pounce on their prey. The eyes were framed with a big pair of glasses and a head of long, wavy black hair. She jumped up to greet him and flashed a smile, making Charlie feel he was a long-lost relative, rather than her next meal! That, or the huge smile was her attempt to offset and distract Charlie from her lack of size. Whichever reason, he instantly felt good being there. She asked if he'd like a drink. As quick as he answered, she was shouting to a staff member to make teas.

This first minute in Yana's company gave him a positive impression of her. One of someone who was quick in nature and got straight to the point of something. Even if the only proof of this was her arranging a prompt cup of tea. The sight of her reminded him of once being told, "If you want a job done, ask someone who's busy." He decided to show plenty of enthusiasm about his project to build a house, so that he'd be taken seriously. After the two sat down at a coffee table, he briefed Yana on his plan.

In response and by default, she produced marketing material of real estate for sale. She asked him to consider an off-plan property, too. He looked at brochures just long enough to show politeness before restating his request to build. Again, as quick as a flash she stood up and called out to a young woman by the name of Elena to come into the room. Yana explained the scenario to Elena, who in turn told Charlie of her uncle being a reputable builder.

He thought, "Brilliant, I'm with two gorgeous women in a room filled with lovely perfume and one of them is related to a reputable builder." Impressed with Yana's speed and ease with providing a solution to his grand plan, he thought, "Mm... I wonder, could this wonder woman solve other puzzles. Like, how to stop foxes rubbing up against my rosemary bush and nearly breaking it." By the end of the meeting, arrangements had been made for him to fly out and meet her uncle.

Charlie thanked them and left the office with a real spring in his step. In fact, so much so, after turning into a quiet side street he jumped and clicked his heels out of spontaneous joy. "Definitely a Mr. Funble and not Mr. Grumble today," said Charlie while smiling! As he walked further from the office, thoughts of work came to mind. They jostled with his reflections on Bulgaria for attention and they won. He had been back in London a couple days and realised that he now needed to focus on his work. Swinging his legs out of bed the next morning, he stared at his new Bulgarian mat on the floor in front of him and said, "No, don't," realising any further staring at it and reflection on Bulgaria would make him late for work. A week prior to leaving for his trip, he had signed a contract to start a house loft conversion and needed to check up on progress. Scaffolding was being erected, so nothing much inside the house was being done. One of Charlie's men – Andy – was also there to oversee anything that might need attention with the clients or scaffolders.

Charlie thought of himself a good boss because he understood the mindset of the working man. He was a forty-four-year-old tradesman and had been in the company of similar people a long time. Long enough to be able to avoid any potential conflicts which arose in working environments. He described himself as a man who went from O-level to a spirit level! Believing in leading by example, he would often work alongside his workers to create a good harmony; and to mitigate any possible strains of a boss and employee working relationship.

He had only pushed the doorbell when the front door was opened by Ms Belcher. "Hello Charlie, you're back, how was the wedding?" she enquired.

At that moment, he realised he had told Andy and Ms Belcher two different stories for his absence. Andy was told he had gone to a funeral and Charlie had told Ms Belcher he was going to a wedding. He wanted to keep his Bulgarian business to himself and didn't mention it to anyone in the workplace. So, this was the reason for his subterfuge. However, giving two different and false reasons for his trip was not intentional and he had forgotten about it until now.

"Hi Charlie, how did the funeral go?" asked Andy after hearing him talking downstairs. He was leaning out of the upstairs loft hatch at a very precarious angle. His head so red and flushed it could almost light paper. Ms Belcher spoke again before Charlie could answer Andy. "You told me you were going to a wedding," she said, leaning forward with a querying look.

Thinking quickly, Charlie said, "Yes, it's true, but there was a funeral the same day. At the time I didn't know which I should go to and in the confusion, I mistakenly told you and Andy different stories."

"Ah how unusual, to be invited to a wedding and a funeral on the same day," replied Ms Belcher. She stressed the 'and' to let Charlie know she had doubts about his story. She continued, "I hope both parties weren't related. Would have been a conflict of choice in deciding." Then, still wearing a sceptical look she asked, "So, which did you choose?"

"Well, after a long, hard think about both occasions I decided I best go to the wedding. You see, you can get a rebuke from a live person for not attending their occasion, but you can't from a dead person!"

"Haha, clever Charlie," said Andy with his face even brighter red from still precariously leaning out of the loft hatch.

"Seriously though, no, I went to the funeral as I thought it right and proper. Besides, if she divorces, I can always go to her next marriage, if there'll be another," he said with gallows humour. While everyone laughed, a sense of relief washed over him from his deft handling of the potentially embarrassing situation. He felt much like a fish wriggling free from a hook and line to be able to swim again!

As with any new introductions between people, mannerisms and habits were keenly observed in the early moments. So too it was in the case of Andy's time with Ms Belcher and husband while Charlie was absent. He enthusiastically told Charlie his observations seen over the previous week. Both agreed that 'unique' was a polite word to use in describing the couple.

They were around sixty years of age, meaning they were biologically mature – though that was all. Mentally, they were more immature, and Ms Belcher had mental problems. Their names were Dick Fruit and Sue Belcher. She always liked to be addressed as 'Ms Belcher'. Her mail was also addressed accordingly. She had delusions of grandeur which she wasn't qualified to possess. Her very poor and unremarkable background didn't entitle her to act snobbish, aloof and often hostile to normal society. She was a huge contradiction and irony with Christmas always provided a glaring proof. She put Advent candles on her front room window sill for anyone passing the house to see, the contradiction being that the couple never put a foot inside a church. A well-disguised, passive hatred of neighbours came naturally to her. As though that wasn't enough to tarnish a character, she suffered from a severe case of regression. Voices of her younger self visited her. Sometimes she saw images of her youth in others, too. Altogether, it made a complex and unpleasant sight accompanied by spontaneous outbursts. The visits from her past youth tormented her and would come unhindered and at will! The result was some embarrassing scenes.

Her unhappiness with herself was visible to anyone engaged with her in the day to day of life. She looked persecuted by another problem, an identity crisis. She regretted and despised her past farmyard youth in a tiny Derbyshire village. Deciding to keep both her illness and personality disorder secrets, Dick was left to find out for himself. They never spoke about her illness when Dick became aware of it. They rather settled for a mutual understanding of it and managed it between themselves. However, at times, good fortune appeared to give her warning of some impending visits from her past. Meaning that she could at least prepare to smother or restrict the effects of the demons on their approach. That ability was most helpful during her younger years of social climbing. Though now and unfortunately, that earlier mental sharpness and strength to contain it had weakened. As a result, clear unhindered mental visions of her unsophisticated youth would come to squat in her mind unchallenged and unannounced. For uncomfortable lengths of time, too.

In the public gaze, she was usually well dressed and performed every mannerism of a well-bred lady. Smelt like flowers in a breeze, her handbag arm held majestically high at right angles. The better for showing off the latest fashion in bags. Then to compliment it, her head was held high alongside. Finally, to complete the act, a mock humble bow of the head would be made at times when any public was in proximity. Though really it was a ploy, cunningly used to avoid any need to speak with someone. She had no time for any pleasantries such as 'good morning' or 'good evening'. She only said them if strongly obliged. Altogether, it was a well-practised and executed performance for the public side of her day-to-day life!

In the privacy of her back garden and out of public sight, she discarded the act to relax. However, with her guard relaxed, it allowed her demons to visit and torment her. Knowing she was defenceless; they would take full advantage before striking hard. Their devilment changed her into an unrecognisable being. She dressed in jeans pulled halfway up her back with seams at bursting point, her body stooped and head swinging from side to side in time with her every lurch. Her movement was not dissimilar to a farmer walking through freshly ploughed fields. Thick straight hair grown long swayed like a wet teacloth in the wind. Farting would often commence along with spitting and blowing snot from her nose. She'd squeeze one nostril closed with a finger, before firing the snot out of the other. (Similar to a workman with filthy hands, being too dirty to rummage a pocket for a handkerchief). Then, the action would finish with her wiping nose with a manicured hand, its wrist bejewelled with bracelets. Snot and bracelets sat uncomfortably together at times! The worse was to come! Bouts of her regression would attack unannounced and manifest itself vocally. She'd start arguing with herself and say, "Leave me alone, go away," speaking as her present self. Only for her to reply to herself with "No, fuck off, you go away, I want to be me again." Then a further reply with "No, I'm me, you're not me any longer, you go away." This back-and-forth conversation between her past and present selves was shock theatre.

As Sue aged, her hair became a metaphor for her personality. During her younger years, her hair was always completely dyed in glorious colours to disguise her true colour. Though now, the roots were more and more visible, showing her true colour.

Then there was Dick – the husband! The man with probably the loudest sneeze! He'd make an awful vocal explosion and no need for it. Though at least the noise of a sneeze is understood, which was unlike anything spoken. Very few understood what he said. Such behaviour was often the case of people with nothing to say. They atoned by either laughing loudly and hysterically at anything said by others. Or, to make loud sneezing as in Dick's case. The loud sneezing was also used as a tactic to draw attention to himself. The two were attention seekers. Though the most noticeable thing about him was his voice and accent. Often, it was one or the other on which people remarked, but seldom both. In Dick's case, both elements of his speech were so strange that it created instant comical remarks by anyone hearing it. The reason being, Dick sounded like a duck quacking when speaking! Even more so when stressed. In such situations, his voice would be indistinguishable from a duck's. Their neighbours next door had a pond in the garden with real ducks and created instant humour. Andy recalled to Charlie how, on one sunny day, the real ducks were actively quacking. Dick was in the garden reading and Sue was in the kitchen. On hearing the ducks quack, she shouted to him through the open kitchen window, "What did you say?"

Then, on another occasion, Dick was in the garden and talking on his phone. The ducks next door could be heard quacking as though replying to him. One time when he and his neighbour were speaking over the fence, the subject of the ducks arose. The neighbour remarked how irregular his ducks quacked. Some days they would be very talkative and others not so much. Dick said how any time he was talking in the garden the ducks seemed very chatty – or quacky. It was at that moment the full realisation dawned on the neighbour of what was happening. How the vocal similarity of Dick and the ducks made the ducks quack when hearing Dick speak. Dick didn't realise it at all.

Sometime later, the neighbour decided to mention the peculiarity to Sue. He felt he knew her well enough not for it to be taken as too pertinent. They both discussed the strangeness of it all and the neighbour laughed hard about it, anticipating Sue would laugh too. She didn't, and instead, gave the neighbour a chastising look.

However, and despite this, the neighbour noticed the conversation triggered a stare from her. She had turned to face the window and look into the distance in silence. Then, the silence was broken by her sternly saying, "Hypothetically, I wonder if one was to be removed, would it be Dick or the ducks?" The neighbour dared not answer because he loved his ducks. Any obligation to reply was undone because Sue spoke again. Slowly and coldly, she said, "Definitely Dick, your ducks are much nicer to look at and they stay outdoors all year!" She gave a crazed laugh immediately after the comment. Dick's last noticeable trait was a snobbery matching Sue's.

Charlie quickly excused himself to climb into the loft and distance himself from Ms Belcher. He gave a sigh of relief while looking at Andy and felt released from her inquisition. The two stood still, Charlie happy his integrity remained intact from his near faux pas with her.

"Charlie, she's not just suspicious, but desperate and wanton too, if you know what I mean," said Andy.

"Oh yeah, why so?"

"When the scaffolders were here, she took a fancy to a big, muscly, quiet one. She kept making excuses to talk with him and acted girly. When they finished erecting the scaffolding and ready to leave, he told me she paid them in cash and gave the money to him. Now, you know how women sometimes spray a love letter with a dash of perfume?"

"Yes, that's right."

"Well, she had sprayed the money with perfume, giving a big sign she fancied him."

"I see. Where was Dick while all this went on?"

"I don't know, drinking, or worried about the increasing levels of competing testosterone. Or maybe searching for his muscles and looking up gym equipment."

"Ha, so did the scaffolder say anything?"

"Not to her but he came to me and said the money reeked of perfume. He said jokingly how it was dosed in it and asked did she run a brothel. Thinking the money came from one of her 'working girls'."

"Seriously? Phew, she wouldn't want to hear that!" The two put hands over their mouths for fear of Sue hearing them.

Next his phone rang, and it was Yana from BG Living. "Hello Charlie, this is Yana from BG Living, how are you?" she said.

"Fine, fine," said Charlie as he gestured leaving the house for privacy.

Yana continued, "Good. Listen, I have some news. Elena has spoken with her uncle about your planned meeting. They are wondering can you go next week to meet him?"

Without hesitation, Charlie said, "Yes, no problem and thank you for arranging this."

"You're welcome, Elena will meet you there and she'll introduce you to her uncle and translate for you as he doesn't speak English too well. I'll speak with you later about your travel day and meeting arrangements."

Nothing but the roof falling in on Charlie would stop him from another trip to Bulgaria, no matter how soon after his first visit. Besides, a meeting with Elena's uncle was always in the planning, albeit a little sooner than Charlie had expected. He walked back into the house and stayed another hour. Then, making his excuses, he left. The intrepid Englishman had a flight to book.

He landed at Sofia International Airport for his second time after a long delay on the runway in London. Again, like the first trip, he was filled with anticipation of what lay ahead with the meeting. Standing up to take his hand luggage out of the overhead storage, he stole a look at the woman still seated next to him, his mind cast back to the awkward delay in London.

Before taking-off, the plane was stationary for an hour and passengers understandably grew restless. The atmosphere in his part of the plane grew particularly tense because of the actions of a woman seated next to him. Her irritation at the delay increased so much that she became very ill-tempered. So much so, that, along with abusing the flight hostesses, she demanded to be left off the plane to have a cigarette. Getting run over by a plane while smoking a cigarette would have been an extreme case of smoking being bad for one's health. Charlie saw the whole thing as a wonderful pantomime and thought of 'stoking the fire' for fun.

When a brief calm took place between spoken diplomacy from the hostesses and verbal abuse from the passenger, he saw his chance. He suggested to the woman she should ask for champagne and a meal from the flight crew as compensation for the excessive delay. However, the 'pantomime' was briefly interrupted by the captain's PA system with an announcement. All passengers suddenly sat up attentively and presumed a take-off was very imminent. Even Charlie's vexed neighbour relaxed more.

Then with a lovely clear accent the captain said, "Good afternoon, ladies, gentlemen and children. Further apologies for our delay. However, I'm happy to announce..." At this very moment in the announcement, the mad woman smiled, expecting the plane to take off soon. The captain continued, "...if anyone with children would like to come up to the cockpit and have a look at the controls, then you're more than welcome. We still do not know when we will..."

He didn't get a chance to finish his announcement when the crazy one exploded once more with abuse, shouting, "Are we ever going to fucking take off?" Her hair and saliva were the only things flying. She eventually calmed down again, and the plane finally took off.

The plane landed at Sofia and Charlie disembarked with his – now calm – neighbouring passenger close behind. Walking to arrivals, he reflected on the pre-flight chaos and felt sorry for her. Such a particular delay was tough on a smoker. They both had an interesting chat when the plane was finally in the air and Charlie found her to be an intelligent Bulgarian woman living in London. She asked if he would like to exchange telephone numbers so they could meet up.

When Charlie politely declined, she offered again, to which he agreed. He wrote 'Hurricane' for her name in his mobile phone address book. Saying goodbye at the passport control and wishing her well, he thought, "Mm, who knows, I may actually call her." As he approached the sliding doors of the arrival's hall, he felt the onset of impending doom. On the other side of the doors would be several desperate taxi drivers eagerly looking to secure a lift from emerging passengers. The airport was a huge magnet for them. Their steely determination in making the best day's wage was very apparent. He remembered his first arrival and how they would grab his arm to secure his business. It almost bordered on harassment. It made him feel like a food parcel being dropped into a highly populated third-world village and everyone wanting a piece of it. Though this time he could prepare his exit better and decided to wait until all passengers from his flight had left the terminal. That way he could slip out and over to the 'OK Taxi' unnoticed and unimpeded.

Well, that was the plan and that was not what happened. When he finally appeared in arrivals, he saw just as many taxi drivers waiting. It resulted in him attracting even more attention from being the only remaining passenger. When he did make it to the 'OK Taxi' kiosk, he looked at the controller, expecting congratulations on his successful navigating of the melee. Instead, he was faced with an expressionless woman who was obviously used to seeing the daily scenes at Terminal One. Requesting a lift, he was then shown to a car. Sitting into the front seat, he thought of Andy back in London and his "Haha, clever Charlie," comment from the loft. He wouldn't be saying that if he had just seen Charlie's badly handled arrival.

He was now starting the last leg of his journey. Before the driver started the engine, Charlie confirmed he was going to the right destination by asking for Pazetahra. The driver replied with a single word "*Da*," signalling to Charlie that he probably didn't speak English. This suited him fine as it eliminated any pressure for conversation as he just wanted to sit back and let his mind drift during the drive. He possessed a fertile mind and liked to dream. When the sights and distractions of Sofia City had passed by, they entered the open country, Charlie closed his eyes and allowed his mind to drift. It wasn't long before he nodded off and the following scene appeared in his mind.

A man walked into a hotel and proceeded along the foyer towards a bar in the distance. Two other men were standing at the bar and talking. The lone man stopped at the bar to order a drink and overheard the other two's conversation.

"So, which do you prefer then?" said one man.

"Oh, I think the Elegances are best," said the other.

"Mm, for me, it's got to be the Regal, nicer and not as expensive as Elegances," said the first man.

"Yes, okay, but Elegances are easier to get hold of and nicer to hold." The man overhearing was perplexed and tried to guess what they were talking about. He stole a look to try help with an answer. The two men were very well dressed, and their hands manicured. He guessed they are probably wealthy and noticed they had no wedding rings. So, he told himself they were talking about the best hotels for prostitutes!

As soon as he came to that conclusion, the reality of the conversation became apparent. One of the men said to the other, "Here, try one, I bet you'll see I'm right," while offering the other man... a cigarette! The cigarette packet had 'Regal' written on it.

Charlie was awakened by the car going over some potholes. He didn't know where he was, but the dream was clear in his mind. He wondered, did he have it at the start of his journey from Sofia, or was it nearer to Pazetahra?

Then the driver said, "*tuk, tuk*" meaning 'here, here' while pointing ahead to a settlement. All became clear now, for he was about to enter the builder's hometown. He assumed it was market day because any car he looked at was fully loaded inside with vegetables. They were squeezed up against all the windows and roof, only leaving the windscreen free. It was busy with convoys of farmers arriving for market day. They came into town from different entry roads with traffic stopping and starting from the congestion. Charlie would rest his gaze on farmers at their steering wheels. Their bodies pushed up against them, from huge piles of vegetables weighing on their backs. Many had ruddy faces, making them look like one of the big tomatoes they were bringing to sell. He smiled at the thought of how, on an overcast day, tomatoes and faces were nearly indistinguishable. The two snaked their way further into Pazetahra and finally to his hotel. He paid and thanked the driver, before stepping into the hotel and heading for his room.

After a short rest on the bed, he went back outside to explore a little more and have some food. As with any new place, his eyes and ears were alert to anything peculiar or particular to a place. Charlie saw a bagpipe player and thought it strange, so he stood to watch and listen for a while. The image looked familiar, but the music sounded different from what he usually heard from bagpipes. "Strange how such an instrument is played thousands of miles from its origins. Maybe it arrived here through the military or roaming tribes, way back," he thought.

As he strolled away from the centre, he saw another sight which triggered his curiosity. It was a group of women in top designer clothes with matching accessories. Gucci and Versace handbags hung off their arms while they chatted and smoked. Every so often they tottered on flashy high heels, their heads occasionally thrown backwards from fits of laughing. It was an anomaly which puzzled him. He saw enough of the town to see it was a working-class one. The group looked to be local country women yet were clad with very expensive designer clothes. Further concentration on the women and their clothes gave him a certain recall. He was once told about the huge business in fake expensive brands in Bulgaria. "Mm, I bet that's it," he thought. After having some dinner and returning to his hotel, he slept and woke up to a new day in Pazetahra. It was the day he'd eagerly been awaiting since that call from Yana in London.

Chapter 4

Elena flew to Bulgaria to meet and take Charlie to her Uncle Borka. A breakfast meeting was planned in which the two men would discuss everything involved in a house build. At the end, hopefully a contract would be signed. All three met at the entrance of a restaurant which was carved out of a mountain. It was most unusual to Charlie. His gawking up at the mountain above the entrance captured Borka's attention. He fixed Charlie with a stare until he lowered his head, then put his hand out and said, "Hallo."

"Hello Borka, thank you for meeting me," replied Charlie. All three entered with only Charlie having to stoop slightly to avoid the head of the entrance. The ceiling inside was higher but not by much. He walked behind Borka, which allowed him an early chance to study the man unnoticed.

He had a long mullet haircut, making him look very 1980s. He was short, too, but with impressive broad shoulders. The restaurant was cavernous and felt like a predator's den. Borka suited the venue, seeing as he looked like a caveman. Charlie hoped it wasn't an ominous sign that he – rather than the menu – was to become Borka's breakfast. The fact that he was in his domain wasn't lost on Charlie. The confidence gained from dealing with business on home territory favoured Borka. Especially when discussions on the price arose. A waiter approached all three and ushered them to a table. Borka sat at the head of it, with Elena and Charlie sitting either side. Looking at him again, Charlie struggled to see any neck, but his chest – like his shoulders – was impressive. With arms outstretched in front and resting on the table, Borka commanded the waiter to bring three breakfasts. Eventually the business of the house project started. Elena told Charlie she would translate for both. Borka started by talking to Elena without turning to face her, then she translated it to Charlie. Charlie then replied to Borka – still looking straight ahead – and Elena translated. That routine went on for an hour, without Borka looking at Charlie even once.

In his mind, he excused him because he had no neck. "Maybe turning his head to talk is impossible unless he moves his body," thought Charlie. Though it still appeared rude, how no attempt was made by him to make some eye contact. At the end of breakfast and discussions, goodbyes were said and Borka departed. Charlie felt he hadn't understood or gained much from the meeting. There was a very strong sense of it finishing prematurely and without any result. A deflated feeling came over him as he and Elena rose from their chairs to leave. Though it was erased when Elena told him to go to Borka's office for further discussions the next day.

It was Friday morning and Charlie arrived at his office. A secretary ushered him into a room at the back. Glass panels allowed him to view all the goings-on in the office space outside. He could see Borka standing by a desk with two female staff, one either side of him. One was standing upright and the other was leaning on the desk with one arm. It was locked at the elbow to support her leaning body, while the other hand was free to flick through paperwork. It was at this moment his respect for Borka grew. Seeing the office and staff rendered him with a look of success and a man of substance. It made Charlie overlook his slightly caveman look of short body, long mullet haircut and a big belly on short legs. Though the barrel chest in front of broad shoulders was impressive.

However, Charlie's positive revision of his character was again in doubt. For Borka suddenly gave the leaning woman a hard slap on her backside. This was followed with a few intimate words and a big laugh from him. Then, again with the other woman, he gave her a hard slap on her backside with his other hand. No intimate words followed but again he laughed. Charlie was surprised at how the women didn't flinch or yelp at the hard slaps. He countered his thought by telling himself they probably expected it when Borka was in the office. His eyes then focused on their backsides. He saw that nature was generous in providing them with fine, full and shapely rumps. "Great armoury to repel any attack from an arse slapper. Maybe a requirement too for employment in Borka's office," he thought. Arse slapping had nearly disappeared in the western world from the prevalence of political correctness and gender protection, though it seemed not here.

It further intrigued Charlie and provided him with amusing thoughts while waiting for Borka to join him. He compared what he'd just seen to a farmer slapping cows' rear ends, to straighten them in the bays for milking. He mused at the idea the habit might have naturally spread from use on farm animals to the public. Then he pictured crests and emblems seen on welcome signs at roadsides by entrances to towns. Imagining one showing a swinging hand landing on a backside with 'Welcome to Pazetahra' written above.

His foolish thoughts came to an end by Borka entering the room. "Hallo Charlie," said Borka.

"Hello again," Charlie replied. It was nice to hear Borka speak English, no matter how well, as it made his greeting seem more real. He knew Borka had to make eye contact with him too, as they now faced each other across the small table. It would help increase Charlie's faith and confidence in trusting him with a house build – should they agree. Borka sat down in front of him and opened a pad of grid-lined paper. He commenced with questions about size and style, then drew lines and shapes in response to Charlie's descriptions.

Seeing the house come alive on paper made Charlie want to smile. Though he didn't, because he needed to remain businesslike until the discussion of cost was over. Any visible sign of delight might be taken by Borka as a sign of soft character, something Borka might try manipulating to his favour during any specifics. He saw Borka's face close up for the first time too and it qualified as remarkable. A hook nose sat between eyes set far apart. The distance between his eyes made looking at him a little uneasy.

While Borka spoke, Charlie developed a habit of continually switching his look between both of Borka's eyes. It worried him how Borka might become annoyed. Annoyed because of Charlie reminding him his eyes were isolated and not a pair. Then, would Borka – for spite – increase the cost of the project? "Tch! This feels awkward. I know what I'll do, I'll look down at his drawing when he looks at me, then when he looks down, I'll look up at him and then switch again and so on. We can do a visual see-sawing," he thought. To complete Borka's facial profile, a long, neat moustache sat above a tidy narrow beard restricted to his chin. His look was not dissimilar to a pirate from the sixteenth century.

The discussions continued and a final design was agreed. It was to be a traditional Bulgarian house with the top floor overhanging the ground one on all sides. Lots of windows and two right-angled balconies, one on each corner of the top floor. Both balconies allowed access from the three bedrooms and gave unobstructed views of the mountains. A very gorgeous house indeed. The price was also agreed and without much haggling. Not because both players had the same price in mind, rather because of Charlie not wanting to irritate Borka and potentially threatening his commitment to build. He really wanted the house and his compliance with Borka's quote was no compromise. It was within Charlie's pre-determined price range. "Okay, Mr Charlie, come here morning for scaled drawing of house. I do overnight," said Borka in broken English.

"Great, thank you," replied Charlie. Truthfully, he wanted to say how impressed he was with Borka's enthusiasm and capability. However, he didn't, as he thought it better not to overdo the compliments at this early stage. They both stood and shook hands. Charlie wouldn't normally be so ready to shake someone's hand which had recently made contact with two women's arses. However, the uniqueness of this occasion in his life was such that he overlooked it.

Arriving back in London was less emotional this time. It was the second trip and any reflections on Bulgaria didn't linger as long as after the first. It allowed him to switch focus, quickly and clearly, onto the equally important job of the loft.

"Morning Ms Belcher how are you. Duck too, I mean Dick, how is Dick?" asked Charlie quickly correcting himself.

"Fine, fine, must dash, see you later, *ciao*! Oh, I nearly forgot, the toilet door lock is playing up, would you have a look at it sometime?" she replied. Not waiting for Charlie to reply, she walked out as fast as her legs allowed, which was slow. Anyone looking at her could see within seconds her well-practised regal demeanour was compromised by the struggle to walk quickly. She winced from the mild physical discomfort of having to swing one leg in front of the other quicker than usual. Charlie raced upstairs to prolong his view of her from a front window. This was because of his shock and interest at the hideous dress she was wearing. It was white, long, loose and crumpled in design. Its collar was high and splayed out looking like a lamp shade. Or similar to an 'Elizabethan collar' worn by dogs to stop them biting other dogs or people. Finally, large bold black wording covered the whole dress. She looked like a walking newspaper. Charlie wondered what all the writing on the dress read. "Please don't laugh, please don't laugh, please…" he thought jokingly.

Turning round and putting a ladder up against the loft hatch, he climbed into the loft to scan and plan the start of work. A few minutes later he heard Andy arrive and climb the stairs two steps at a time.

"Charlie, did you see her?" he said while climbing into the loft. He continued, "What's that she's wearing? I just passed her coming up from the station. She looks like a walking bag of chips." He was referring to previous times when fish and chip shops wrapped takeaway fish and chip meals in newspaper. "Did you notice the collar? Can you imagine if she starts one of her mad fits of loud talking. That collar will amplify it all over the neighbourhood!"

The two laughed and Charlie said, "That's right, and dogs sometimes have to wear similar collars to prevent them biting other dogs?"

"Hey that's right. Maybe she's run out of medication and scared of what she might do," joked Andy.

"Mm, anyway, Andy, let's get our heads around this," said Charlie in a more serious tone. After measuring for an opening, the two started to work on the back slope of the pitched roof. This was to provide an access for steels to be swung in, which would eventually support the new floor joists. Charlie sometimes worked alongside his men to keep in touch with the physical side of building work, though usually he concentrated on the business side of things.

He left around lunchtime to deal with a Power of Attorney (P.O.A.) for Borka. The purpose of which, to allow someone to act on behalf of a client in their absence. He went into the job next morning without having been able to obtain the P.O.A. Ms Belcher had left a key for him in the hall the previous day. It gave him independence to come and go as he pleased. As he approached the stairs, he heard her talking with a woman. He stopped for a moment to listen better and heard the following. "Now, I don't allow too much talking on mobile phones and smoking in the house. That goes for the garden and outside the front too. The sight of someone smoking outside the front cheapens the look of a house. So, you must tell me now whether you smoke."

"No, I don't smoke," came the reply.

Craning his neck forward with head tilted sideways, like a bird looking for a worm in the ground, he waited to hear more. The pause was too long and he thought it best to keep moving, in case of being caught listening. He made it to the second step when the woman walked into the hall and the two looked at each other.

"Oh my God, it's that mad woman who was on my delayed flight," he thought. He gave no visible sign of recognising her and she did the same. So, neither knew if one had recognised the other. It would remain a mystery to each of them for the time being, because Charlie said nothing and quickly climbed the stairs. He decided it best, in case Ms Belcher appeared. A delay might have led to introductions and an obligation by Charlie to admit knowing the woman. That would then provide a chance for her possibly telling Ms Belcher about their meeting on a flight to Bulgaria. Hearing that would set off an alarm bell in Ms Belcher's head about Charlie's integrity with telling the truth. Meaning, she might suspect Charlie was lying about going to a funeral or wedding instead of Bulgaria. Any thought of such behaviour would damage their working relationship. Client trust and satisfaction were of utmost importance to Charlie, so too for the client.

In the safety of the loft, he pondered over that value, also about why the woman was here in the house. He could now hear Ms Belcher speaking to the woman. The tone of her voice sounded as though she was instructing her. Later, he found out she was the new cleaner.

The following day, he arrived on the job with the intention of having a chat with the cleaner. He wanted to tell her he remembered her from that delayed flight. This would avoid any future awkward moments from them pretending not to know each other. Also, to ask her if she knew any Bulgarians in London from the legal profession to provide his P.O.A. She arrived not long after him and they finally chatted in the upstairs hall while Ms Belcher sat in the garden. "Hello again," said Charlie.

"Hello," she replied.

"I just want to say, I do remember you and I'm sure you recognise me too – yes?"

Smiling, she said, "Yes I do, and I'm embarrassed about my outburst on that flight."

"Ah, don't worry yourself about it. It would have been worse if there was absolutely no reason to show temper. Anyway, sorry but I've forgotten your name."

"Nelly," she said.

"Nice name. Listen, how will you deal with her smoking ban? I overheard Ms Belcher telling you smoking isn't allowed. You'll go crazy if you can't smoke!" he asked.

"I'll go to the toilet, lock the door and blow the smoke out the window,"

"Mm, okay, but be careful, don't get caught. She's what we English would describe as a prig. It means easily irritated or upset."

Nelly smiled and said, "Ah you mean like me then, when I'm on a delayed flight? Why do you call such people a pig?"

"Ha, no I wouldn't and didn't say that, I said prig – with an 'r'," he replied.

"Ah I see. About the flight, I think I was entitled to be upset from that delay. Also, I think prig is too polite a word to describe her. Maybe pain in the ass is more accurate, a pig's ass, too – you think?"

The two just managed to stifled part of their joint laughter so Ms Belcher wouldn't hear, and Charlie followed it up by quickly asking, "Look, I nearly forgot to ask you, do you know any legal Bulgarians in London?" She burst out laughing as couldn't contain it. His question being asked so quickly after their previous laughing made Nelly instantly laugh again. She automatically took it as a joke because their present mood was one of ridiculing Ms Belcher. However, Charlie wasn't laughing after his question, and Nelly quickly realised he was serious. Raising her eyes an inch and dropping her voice an octave, she replied with a curt voice, "What do mean, any legal Bulgarians in London?"

"Tch, no sorry, I mean, any Bulgarian professional legal people in London, you know, to do a Power of Attorney for me?" he replied while smiling at her misunderstanding.

After her swift change of expression from shock to relief, Nelly said, "Ahh yes, I do, my cousin may be able to help, she is on the Bulgarian Embassy Register of Translators. Maybe she can recommend."

"Brilliant, any suggestion will help. What's her name?" After Charlie took the name, the two parted because they heard Ms Belcher coming into the house.

An enquiring call of "Nelly, where are you?" was heard by both.

"I'm upstairs, Ms Belcher," Nelly replied. She busied herself with speedier cleaning, by way of redeeming herself for just having mocked Ms Belcher.

The working day passed by, and Charlie left the house to search on the Bulgarian Embassy website for Nelly's cousin. Her name was Lubka and he found her contact details. He then called to arrange translations and notarizing of the documents. Unfortunately, she couldn't do the notarizing. Notaries charged a lot of money for a signature and Charlie wanted to avoid it if possible. Thankfully he discovered the Bulgarian Embassy signed official documents for a reasonable fee. Delighted to have solutions in place, he posted the P.O.A. to her and received them back with all the translations. Off he went to the Bulgarian Embassy for the signatures the next day. Queuing was usually boring and tedious but not this queue. A motley line of characters stood in it and one man provided some fun to break the monotony of queuing. His photo for a visa or passport was refused by the counter staff and he asked, "What's wrong with it? That photo is only a week old,"

"Yes, sir, but it's not very clear and slightly blurred. Where was it taken?"

"Prague on a stag night. You should have been there, it was great," he replied.

The staff member remained unsurprised at the man's recount of the photo's origin and simply replied, "Well sir, you'll have to produce another clearer photo with proper specifications – sorry,"

"Tch, I should have got a copy of the police one taken of me after my arrest, that would've been okay – wouldn't it?"

The man behind the desk finally broke his statuesque expression and raised his eyebrows. Stifled laughter and mutterings came from some in the queue.

Back on the job, steel had arrived and was placed in position during those days. Nelly appeared once more, as she worked two days a week in the house. One day when stepping out of the loft, he saw her looking up at him from the hall. "Hi Nelly, are you okay?" he asked.

"Hi Charlie, you know this woman is crazy, don't you?" she replied.

His intuition told him Nelly might have seen one of Sue's mad outbursts as he thought what else would cause her to say 'crazy'. Even so, he didn't give any clue he might know and only said, "What do you mean?"

"You know me and my cigarette? Well, I went to the toilet to have a quick smoke while she was in the garden. I had the window open and things okay, until I tried to open the toilet door and leave. It wouldn't open."

Charlie instantly remembered being asked to fix the latch on the toilet door and that he hadn't done so.

She continued, "It wouldn't open, so I stood on the toilet to lean out of the window to call Ms Belcher to come help me. I shouted, 'Ms Belcher, I can't get out of the toilet.' She then said, 'Fuck off, leave me alone.' This is mad and strange for a lady to say, no?"

Charlie's eyes closed from smiling so hard and he barely managed to smother an oncoming laugh. Nodding his head, he said, "Yes, yes, I know, but carry on."

Nelly continued, "Anyway, I called out to her again and she said something like, 'Go away, I'm not you anymore, I'm me, or something like that. What is her problem, is she loony because no one else in the garden, just her? Is she safe to be around?"

After climbing down the ladder, he put his hand on her shoulder. Like a mentor would do with their charge while enlightening them about something. Smiling again, Charlie explained to Nelly about mad Sue. "Nelly, let me explain. She has a bit of a problem, and she talks to herself sometimes. I won't go into it now but just treat her condition as amusing and not directed at anyone, then it won't bother you. Besides, wait until you see the husband. His name is Dick, and he talks like a duck,"

"Oh no, what a strange couple. We have a place in Bulgaria where we put such people," she replied.

"Here also, but that's another subject," he said. Then, turning to look towards the garden, he said, "You know, I'm just thinking, it's the wrong one who's talking to themselves. It should be Dick because only he understands himself, oh, except for the ducks next door,"

"What, the ducks next door? What's that about?" asked an increasingly perplexed Nelly.

"Oh later, Nelly. Listen, I must go somewhere tomorrow, so I'll see you in a few days," he said.

Charlie touched down at Sofia International Airport for his third time. Borka had started building his house and Charlie wanted to see how his dream was materialising. When first told about the commencement of works, he felt ennobled. Ennobled from his decision to add something to the earth's surface. He knew it was only a house but nonetheless, it was a new addition and permanent fixture on planet earth. A representation of himself and giving him a sense of achievement. A permanent mark and legacy of his presence.

His journey from the airport started with a pleasant surprise this time. Instead of driving straight to Bonkas, the driver suggested a trip to Rila Monastery. It was a small detour at the early part of his journey from Sofia. Charlie vaguely knew about the monastery and welcomed the suggestion for a cultural excursion. Also, the driver would make some extra money from the detour. Both were happy. While on their way, he was consumed with thoughts of the house and the need to see it. So much so that he considered cancelling the Rila trip to reach Ovineshta quicker. However, he didn't and was later glad for it.

As the monastery came into view, curiosity and anticipation grew within Charlie. On entering the complex he was immediately impacted by the enormity of it and felt very small, like an ant in a huge sink. The door through which he entered was disproportionately small and didn't prepare him for the vastness beyond. The atmosphere within the walled compound appeared to weight and push on him. It was disorienting, too, making him a little dizzy and finding it surreal. The Rila monastery is a huge open-top four-sided building. Several floors rise to a great height with continuous balconies circling each floor. It houses monks and was a refuge for those hiding from foreign rulers in the past. It's a popular pilgrimage site for Orthodox Christians, some of whom come and stay in its rooms to pray and contemplate. Its height and dramatic design makes it slightly imposing for anyone in the courtyard looking up. Altogether, its parts made a unique experience for the senses. Before leaving, he saw a church or chapel within the grounds. Its door was open and allowed the shinning gold iconography to be seen by anyone outside.

It was mid-afternoon when he arrived in Bonkas. He decided to stroll around town and take the opportunity of having a massage that evening. His hotel had a spa centre, and it seemed a waste not to make use of it. Refreshed for the morning, he went to Ovineshta to take his first look at his materialising house. He told the driver to drop him off one hundred metres from his plot, so he could approach it on foot. A slow approach allowed him to prepare for what he was about to see. Getting out of the taxi and taking his first few steps, he felt apprehensive. "I hope it doesn't look too small against all this open countryside. Mm, I wonder how many workers are there?" he thought. Sensing he was very near; he slowed his walk so the sight of the house would gradually come into view. This first sight of it was special and he wanted to experience it gradually.

Finally, there he was, standing still and looking at it in the near distance. "Wow, look at that!" he whispered. He had no immediate opinion formed of what he saw, only that it looked the right shape, looked strong and was upright. It was a unique experience for him as he had no previous one with which to compare it. Though it didn't matter too much at that point because of other overriding emotions and thoughts. They were a sense of achievement at being able to initiate something large to rise from the ground.

"All mine and what a fantastic sight," he gushed. The house was in the shell stage, meaning only the external walls and roof were erected. A roofer had only started tiling it. "I won't go inside or disturb him, but will come back later when he's gone home," he thought.

Returning in the early evening, he stepped inside and was still overjoyed with it. He stood staring out at the Pirin mountains through the opening for the front door. They looked magical. Then, to prolong and expand the wonderful view, he stepped backwards to the opposite wall. The view of the mountains filled every window space, along with the door opening. It was as though the foothills were just outside the door. The apparent proximity of house to mountains was mesmerising. The other incredible view to savour was from the upstairs floor. Again, it was magical. Standing well back from an unfinished balcony, he marvelled at the Pirin Mountains.

That, together with the sun, blue sky and wholesome smell of the countryside, made a perfect moment.

Then sudden without warning, that perfect idyll was interrupted by a sound of someone entering the house. He heard heavy breathing and a walking stick stabbing the floor every few seconds. It made Charlie anxious, and he envisaged someone deranged climbing the stairs of his house. Walking to the stairs and looking over the handrail, he saw a tall elderly man with a huge grin on a baby face staring up at him. "Hello?" said Charlie. The man replied with something in Bulgarian. He continued to move around the ground floor stabbing it with his stick while looking and examining the interior.

Charlie descended the stairs to meet him and heard him say, "*Evro*." Then, he rubbed his thumb and index finger together while staring at Charlie to gauge any reaction. Again, he said "*Evro*," while smiling.

"Ha, he's some character. I must get him out of here because he's putting marks in the floor with his walking stick," thought Charlie. Walking outside to draw the man away from the house, Charlie smiled and tried to speak a few Bulgarian words he knew. The man still grinned, then raised his stick to point over to his wife in the next field. As he walked away, he beckoned Charlie to follow him. He did and on meeting her was treated to a traditional Bulgarian song. She had no teeth, smooth skin and wore a traditional white head scarf. She was tall for a woman too, good-looking, and her husband stood by her side. Together, they stood side by side with the Pirin Mountains in the background. Charlie felt as though he had walked into a promotional video for The Bulgarian Tourist Board. The husband continued to grin, while she sang, and Charlie listened. The breeze even appeared well behaved by not blowing too strong to drown her voice. It was only when nearing the end of the song, Charlie thought there might be more symbolism to it. Bulgaria had so many rituals and traditions that the song could be a welcome or blessing for his new house. The consideration was just made in time for him to make an extra effort in applauding them. He shook their hands and said, "*Blagodaryia.*"

Charlie gestured to them he would leave his lovely new neighbours and friends. Though before he could depart, the husband put a finger up in the air as though to delay Charlie. Taking a pen and piece of paper out his pocket he wrote '2 leva = 1 evro' and pointed to Charlie's house. He finished the sequence with a knowing smile. Charlie had earlier ignored his repeating of the word 'evro' but understood some Bulgarians pre-occupation with the currency exchange rate. It was rumoured they might adopt the currency sometime in the future like many East European countries. Others would follow, so there was a mild fascination with the 'euro'.

Looking down at the piece of paper, Charlie smiled and said a compliant "*Da, dobre.*" Then, just before looking away, he thought the paper's size and texture looked familiar. He used the breeze as an excuse to hold a flapping corner. Doing so gave him an opportunity to turn it over to see what was on the other side. He did and was shocked to see his own picture! It was the police poster of himself standing by the stolen taxi. "Crikey, that's been lying around a while," he thought. Not wanting to delay any longer, he gestured to the man that he must go and asked if he could keep the paper. Regardless of him knowing he didn't understand him, Charlie took it and shoved it into his pocket. He walked away smiling and waving to the couple.

As he strode further away, he said, "I wonder whether or not they know that's me in the picture?"

Chapter 5

After another visit to the house and another massage, he decided to go back to Sofia for a couple days before his return flight to London. Borka didn't need to see him, and Charlie was up to date with the build. So, he thought it an opportunity to stay a couple days in the capital to look around and discover, rather than just passing through it. He heard about the Alexander Nevsky cathedral and made it his first visit after arranging his hotel. As with all cathedrals, its opulence and beauty was spellbinding. Looking up at the dome immediately dwarfed any earlier grand notion of his new house. The cathedral's place in the list of biggest cathedrals crossed his mind. He made a point of looking it up later. Next, he went onto the cultural centre called NDK and the huge park in front. He sat on a bench for the rest of the day, to soak up the sun and watch people go by. In the moments between anyone passing, he wallowed in pleasant thoughts of future progress with his house.

That evening he decided to have a couple of drinks and settle down somewhere nice. After trying a few bars for comfort, he came upon The Sheraton Hotel. He entered and ordered a beer. Sitting next to him at the bar was a respectable-looking elderly gentleman. He wore a tailored suit and hat. He looked timid and mannerly, and his breast pocket handkerchief drew Charlie's attention. It was carefully placed to show just enough, signalling to him that the man inside the suit was one of good breeding and class. Eventually he leant over to Charlie and spoke. Unfortunately, he couldn't hear him very well and it remained that way for the duration of their conversation. Charlie tried his best to give relevant replies to any partially heard questions and comments. Not wanting to appear rude, he avoided the temptation to request any repeat of a question. He was frustrated at not hearing him properly because one of the few words he did understand was *'Bulgartabac'*. *Bulgartabac* was an old Bulgarian tobacco company, and he guessed the man was possibly a founder or at least related to it in some way. His several mentions of it reinforced that assumption for Charlie. The gentleman stood up to leave and Charlie apologised for not hearing him clearly while wishing him well. He replied with a warm smile and a slight bow of his head. While watching him walk to the doors, he reasoned that the man was possibly happy enough just having someone listen to him.

Straightening his back from previously crouching, he scanned the bar for any other interesting figures. He saw two men further down talking loudly about discovery and findings. Charlie wondered if they were archaeologists because a lot of antiquities were being unearthed in Bulgaria at that time. Headlines were written regularly about amazing gold artefacts being found, particularly in the Thracian region near the Greek border. He soon lost interest because he couldn't hear all of what they spoke. Turning his head once again to look across the bar, his eyes met another pair looking straight at him. They were a nice pair, too, and belonged to a woman. Eyes met long enough for Charlie to be convinced she was interested in him. Next, she got up from her stool and walked around to join him. "I bet she walks out the door," he said while his eyes followed her. "I don't believe it, she's coming towards me," he mumbled. Her walk around the bar was long enough for Charlie to plan what to say. He was overjoyed with the prospect of talking with a woman for the rest of the evening. "Hello, how are you? I saw you speaking with the old man and wondered, were you on holiday, or maybe a business trip? This is central Sofia and such people come and go," she said.

"Hello and good question but neither," he replied. He smiled and anticipated her being surprised when hearing his real reason for being in Bulgaria. He continued, "I'm actually here to build a house."

"Oh really? How wonderful, where?" she asked.

He invited her to sit, offered her a drink and the two continued to talk. He was having the most wonderful time and saw she was, too. They spoke, laughed and contemplated life through the night. At one point, they were speaking about books, writers and reading. Charlie was no academic or a particularly avid reader, but nonetheless had read a certain amount over the years. She told him she recently left university after studying Classics. He highlighted Oscar Wilde as being an interesting read and talked about the writer having been Irish. He knew Wilde had studied Classics too and mentioned it. She gave a reply which made Charlie sit up and set her aside as being someone special in his opinion.

That reply was, "I think he writes in a particularly English style." On hearing it, he thought it unusual how a young Bulgarian should make such an observation. He became even more attracted to her for her saying it. Also, for possessing brains and beauty in equal measures. The night progressed with them not realising three am had arrived and the bar closing. The age-old conundrum of what to do at closing time, when man and woman have just met, bothered Charlie. Wondering how to profit further from her company both intrigued and irritated him. Thankfully he was spared the task of finding the right words to use, for she spoke first saying, "Do you want to go somewhere else now?"

"Great, she's said it for me," he thought. He was about to say, 'yes' when he remembered the time and said, "I guess there're only clubs open now, and won't they be closing soon?"

She rolled her eyes upwards, then lowered them while sighing and said in a business-like manner, "Where is your hotel?" A hollow feeling struck Charlie's stomach on him hearing those four words. Within him, conflicting emotions swirled in his head. One of admiration for her, another of a sense of foolishness for himself. More thoughts of annoyance at being too naïve to spot her ruse, while also having pity for her. A pity for needing to ply the oldest trade in the world. He thought of his house, while she thought of his hotel, as they were ushered out of the bar and to a taxi.

The following afternoon he set out for the airport. She 'sat' in his mind for the whole journey back to London. Conflicting emotions for her wrestled with no outright winner. He tried to reconcile her action of selling herself with her intelligence. The following morning, he was walking up the front footpath of the job. Nelly came out of the house and greeted him. "Hello Charlie, how was your trip?"

"Hello Nelly, mm, interesting," he replied with raised eyebrows while thinking about the woman in The Sheraton Hotel. He had just shaped his mouth to say something again but froze from a sudden surprise thought. He stared past Nelly while realising he hadn't asked that girl for her name. Resetting his mind to the present again, he said, "Anyway, I'll be going back and forth a bit more regularly from now onwards, Nelly. I better go check up on things upstairs."

He had decided earlier to tell Nelly about his venture in Bulgaria for two reasons. Firstly, in the hope she could suggest someone for his P.O.A. Then secondly, he liked the comforting value of having a confidante to speak with about his trips. Even if it was only for her to listen. He knew he had her confidence, too, because he had warned her he'd tell Ms Belcher about her smoking, should she waver. The loft was looking good, with the addition of the new dormer window having been constructed and weathered. All the loft was insulated, too.

A second man was helping Andy, and he went by the name of Tagaby. A strange name and it was only after his explanation that everyone thought it cool. Tagaby was a nickname, instead of his real name of Ray. He was a musician and tried to make success of a band he formed called Tagaby. It was an acronym for 'Take A Gamble And Be Yourself'. Ray believed so many people had an unhealthy preoccupation with how others saw them. It held them back from attempting to fulfil dreams, to discover hidden talents and ultimately succeed. So, he had decided to call his band a name to reflect that philosophy. However, the band wasn't successful and Tagaby was back working in construction.

Andy, on hearing his story reminded Tagaby of the saying, "You can bring a horse to the water, but you can't make it drink."

Tagaby understood but didn't want to agree. His reply was "Mm, I don't know, more a case of 'pearls before swine' regarding my music. The band wasn't appreciated." He did consider starting another band and with the name Talvoby – 'Take A Longer View Of Being Yourself' in hope of that being a success. Though he didn't, as the name was a mouthful and didn't roll off the tongue like Tagaby.

He was a bit of a prankster and had bought a duck whistle to have some fun with Dick and Ms Belcher. He would blow the duck whistle from the scaffolding to hear Ms Belcher say, "Yes, what is it, Dick""

To which he'd reply, "Nothing, I said nothing." The neighbour saw him blowing it one day, but thankfully laughed and didn't tell Dick or Ms Belcher to spoil the fun. He even gestured to Tagaby to blow it whenever seeing him from his garden. Later in the job, Tagaby's joking went further with comical results. He eventually tired of the duck whistle, but another opportunity for a prank would come his way.

His girlfriend had temporarily barred him from their flat over an ongoing disagreement. He needed somewhere for the next few nights and daringly decided to sleep in the loft of the job. It would save money he'd otherwise waste on temporary accommodation. He knew there'd be a reconciliation and looked forward to telling her he didn't waste any money on accommodation. It would make the making-up sweeter. Utmost guile and stealth were required to avoid detection while sleeping in the loft. He knew Charlie would go barmy if he found out. His first night went smoothly. After leaving the job with Andy and parting company, he'd go to a cafe for dinner, then a pub for a pint and read a newspaper. At ten pm, he'd then creep through the side passage of the house and up the scaffolding. After unhooking the tarpaulin covering the dormer window opening, he'd climb through.

Using packages of insulation for a mattress, a rolled-up dust sheet for a pillow and another for a blanket, he bedded down for the night. He never worried about sleeping-in, as he had the good habit of waking up naturally the same time every morning. The next working day passed and again he prepared his nighttime arrangements. While lying and waiting to go off to sleep for his second night, he felt his phone vibrate. It was a message from his girlfriend saying, "*Love you, come home.*" Overjoyed and surprised at the earlier than expected reconciliation, his mind switched to the two downstairs. They went to bed at ten-thirty pm and it was during the following half hour that Tagaby decided to play a prank on them. It was to be his last night and he thought, "*Why not?*"

He waited until three am before creeping out of the loft hatch shoeless, down the stairs and stopping at their bedroom door. Breathing slowly and quietly, he edged closer to it. He raised a fist with its middle finger protruding ready to knock. Looking over his shoulder to check his getaway, he knocked three times, *Knock... Knock... Knock*. Then quickly and quietly, he climbed the stairs to stand out of sight and spy from the landing. Nothing was heard from inside the room. Only after being sure of no one stirring, he again descended the stairs to – again – knock three times. Slightly louder, firmer and spaced further this time.

"Who is it?" roared Ms Belcher. After a three second pause, again she roared, "Who is it?"

Elbowing Dick lying next to her, he stirred from his sleep saying, "What?"

"Did you hear that? Someone is at the door, get out and see," she exclaimed.

"I can't hear anything," whimpered a sleepy Dick. Tagaby heard the two speaking but only understood Sue. He descended to the door once more to knock three times, to make sure Dick had proof. "Oh God, what's that?" quaked Dick after coming to his senses.

"See I told you. Oh my God, she's come for me, she's come for me, help me, God, she's come for me!" she screamed.

"Calm down. Who's come for you?" he quaked.

"My other self, my younger self," she whined.

"Oh no, I can't deal with two of you, one is enough," he replied.

Now wearing a determined face, she bawled, "Get out, I tell you. Get out and see who it is. Are you a man or mouse?"

"Well, apparently I'm a duck according to what I'm overhearing from people around here." Dick had no choice but to climb out of the bed, as she was now kicking him. Slowly he crept towards the door and quickly locked it. "Don t lock it, go outside and see," she demanded.

"Not likely, there could be a madman out there," he replied. Trotting back to the bed, the two pulled the sheets up to their noses and stared at the door. Tagaby was grinning from ear to ear while listening to their petrified reactions, then finally a silence came from the room. He heard Dick locking the door earlier, meaning both wouldn't come out. So, he decided to boldly go into the kitchen to find a quick snack. He was hungry and took the gamble. Fortunately for him, he saw two phones on chargers in the kitchen. It meant they couldn't call the police and Tagaby was safe in staying for the rest of the night. Climbing the stairs with a thick and well-packed sandwich, he bedded down for the remainder of the night.

Andy arrived the next morning to an unusually quiet house. There were no sights or sounds of anyone in morning preparations. Then after a minute or so, Dick and Sue came out of the bedroom wearing night clothes and shocked faces. "Oh my God, what a night. We had a burglar, and it was awfully frightening," she squealed.

"You said it was your younger self visiting," quaked Dick.

"Shut up, I didn't," she retorted.

While looking in the fridge, Dick said, "Anyway, whoever it was has good taste. It's eaten all the foie gras and sourdough bread. A discerning ghost, maybe."

Then Andy said jokingly, "If it was a ghost, you better check your spirits in the drinks' cabinet! Ha, get it – spirits." No one heard him, or if they did, they refused to acknowledge it.

Then, Ms Belcher's eyes widened, and she stared into the distance from a sudden realisation and she said, "Oh my God, I've just thought, who was the previous owner? Didn't she do market research and have people around for meetings?" Then, to everyone's surprise she exclaimed, "I bet the meetings were seances and she spoke with the dead or the devil! Oh my God, oh my God, we'll have to sell. We have a resident ghost or devil," she screamed.

"Calm down, calm down, you'll have one of your fits," said Dick.

By this stage, Charlie and Nelly had arrived and joined the frantic scene. Nelly then said, "You could get a priest to exorcise the house.

"Oh no, absolutely not. I can't have the local priest thinking we have a ghost. The embarrassment would be too much," she replied while wiping a tear.

Nelly was standing in the corner of the kitchen, listening and scheming. She thought it an opportunity to make some extra money and stood forward to suggest getting a Bulgarian priest to perform the exorcism. "Don't worry, Ms Belcher, in Bulgaria we have many ghosts running around the country causing trouble. Government even considered creating a Ghost Minister, it got so bad. That's why we don't have too many fat people. They're always worrying away their fat from thoughts of ghosts suddenly appearing! Listen, Ms Belcher, let me arrange for a Bulgarian priest to come. He won't charge much and will be anonymous to people in the area. He can arrive in ordinary clothes and change into his vestments for the exorcism inside the house." Nelly couldn't tell if Sue and Dick's expressions were ones of shock, disbelief, or of consideration. She had to wait and see if her offer would be taken up.

At that moment the doorbell rang, and Charlie went to the front door. "Hi, I'm Axel, Sue's son," said the caller.

He stepped inside, making Charlie move back from the door. Charlie chose to go upstairs to avoid any further conversation with Axel. There was no need to further engage with him. Despite that, while climbing the stairs he regretted not asking him the reason for his name. He was sure it was a Jewish name, but the family wasn't Jewish.

The truth of it was that Axel was originally named Alex by his parents, but he decided to have it changed to Axel by deed poll. The only reason being that it sounded cool. His tongue – like his shoelaces – was loose and regularly tripped him up. If his hair grew any longer, it'd have done the same. He habitually peppered his conversation with popular foreign phrases, always to ill effect from constant mispronunciation. Like his name, he was an anagram because of his mood swings. His personality fluctuated and was a result of drug use. Also, his disruptive school years from expulsions didn't help. The thirty-five-year-old Axel greeted his mother like a child and pronounced everything wrong. He entered the kitchen.

"Hi mummy, *comment allez-vous?*"

Sue replied with a stare, "Hello darling."

"Is anything wrong?" he asked.

"Oh, don't worry, your mother's just contemplating having the house exorcised," said Dick while raising his eyebrows.

"Wow, cool," replied Axel. Andy left the kitchen and joined Charlie on the upstairs landing. Both secretly listening like children staying up past their bedtime.

"Oh, I noticed someone looking around outside the house, don't know who she is, and the door is open. She's huge and about two metres tall, looks a bit weird too," said Andy.

Charlie skipped downstairs to investigate, "Hello, can I help you?" he said with a quizzical look. The woman looked back at Charlie as though to study him in return. Charlie's expression had irritated her because she walked towards the front door and entered while retorting, "I'm Axel's partner, you knob head."

"Ah sorry," he replied while he watched her waddle down the hall towards the back kitchen. "My word, it's getting stranger by the minute here," he mumbled.

"Hi Sue, what's happenin'?" she bawled.

"Hello Beastie, sorry, sorry, I mean Betsie, nice to see you," Sue embarrassingly replied.

"Listen, Mummy's thinking of getting the house exorcised," Axel quickly exclaimed. It was to save Sue any further blushes from her Freudian slip. A huge volcanic laugh erupted from Betsie. Anyone with the slightest imagination wouldn't be blamed for thinking they were listening to a ship's foghorn.

While Betsie's head was arched back laughing at the ceiling, everyone else gave each other a knowing look. One of mixed embarrassment and confusion about whether Betsie's laugh was from Sue's Freudian slip regarding her name or hearing about an exorcism.

"Wicked, wicked, 'ave you got someone to do it?" she enthusiastically enquired.

"Well, probably yes," said Sue.

"Ah, no wait, let me get you a duppy to free the house of wotever. I can get my grandmuver to send one over from Jamaica, innit?" said Betsie.

"What's a duppy and how much is a flight from Jamaica," a startled Sue asked. Another volcanic laugh raced out from Betsie's inside. "Ha, ha, ha, no, you got it all wrong, Sue innit. A duppy is a spirit and my grandmuver can put it to work for you from Jamaica."

Sue politely refused by saying, "Ah, thank you darling but I'm doubtful and sceptical. Are you sure you're correct in what you say about this duppy thing? I think if I was to go ahead, I'd like to deal with a real person such as a priest. Thank you, anyway."

"Okay, no prob, Sue, your choice," said Betsie.

"Mummy, we gotta go now and check you later – *ciao*," said a restless Axel. They left the house, not knowing Charlie's and Andy's eyes followed their departure from upstairs.

"What do you make of all that? So incongruous," whispered Charlie.

"Phew, that's a big word rarely heard on a building site, Charlie," Andy mockingly replied.

"Seriously though, aren't they a strange bunch?" asked Charlie looking confused and slightly stunned. He continued, "Anyway, he's definitely one to watch."

"Well, you know what they say about Axels – whichever way you spell the word, their wheels can fall off!" replied Andy, feeling clever and looking at Charlie from the corners of wide expectant eyes.

Everyone eventually separated to go about their work or business. Charlie had a few words with Andy in the hall about work. Andy listened but his mind was on what just happened in the kitchen. He said, wearing a cheeky smile, "I wonder, will their council tax be affected by a ghost moving in?"

Charlie replied with a dismissive look but decided to reply in kind by saying, "Hearing Dick mention the missing food made me think of a quack snack rather than a quick snack,"

"Ha, yes I get you," replied Andy. Charlie smiled as he turned away to look for Nelly. He found her alone and told her he was off to Bulgaria again. "Okay, will you get me a bottle of Rakia this time please?" she whispered. He smiled and nodded before slipping away from the house unnoticed.

For the fourth time, Charlie landed in Sofia International Airport. After first visiting his house, he would travel onto Pazetahra to meet Borka for an overnight stay. He guessed Borka's invitation was a customary thing to do by a house builder for their clients. Walking along the lane to his own place in Ovineshta, Charlie was thinking of a name to call it. It was developing into a fine house full of interesting details. The traditional style made it stand out from almost anything else being built in the region. Apartments were the choice for new builds and didn't have the scope to show much design.

Building a four-sided, standalone structure allowed for so much creativity. Also, he knew he would have no – or very little – competition should he want to sell it, simply because of the virtual lack of new houses and only blocks of apartments erected.

A chimney now rose from the roof to vent the wood stove in the downstairs open-plan area. Upstairs, the three bedrooms were finished, and the two bathrooms had suites fitted, the wall and floor tiles yet to be laid. Downstairs, the kitchen remained to be fitted and the decorating throughout the whole ground floor was still to be done. Borka had built a lean-to roof outside one end of the property, over an open-sided patio area. The low end of the roof being supported by posts coming up from the edge of the terrace. Finally, a handrail and balustrades roughly a metre up from the floor completed the picture. The terrace was a continuation of the house's ground floor and was waiting to be slabbed. Then finally, stone cladding had to be fitted on both sides of all four external corners. The idea of that was to break up the continuous white roughcast look of the ground floor walls. Stepping back and looking at it from a short distance, the many windows and two corner balconies did the most to promote its appeal. The overhanging eaves added to its richness too. All the woodwork was painted a dark brown. Of course, there were a few unappealing parts of the house construction remaining. The electricity supply being one, and its fifty-metre trench from house to the connection board to be dug out and later backfilled. Those jobs were for later, but for now, Charlie was pleased with the overall progress and style. He walked further into his plot to distance himself from it, so he could gain a fuller view.

A goat herder walked by with his large herd, the leading goat wearing a bell. The dull and irregular ringing of its bell seemed to be cued to exactly the right time. It gave the perfect accompanying sound to a perfect view. Charlie decided to go back to Bonkas and walked away from the house. He took a last casual sideways look of the Pirins and did a 'double take' because he thought he also saw Mr 'Evro'. He was correct and saw Mr 'Evro' looking back at him from his field while waving. Charlie laughed at the surprise of seeing him and waved back. He was out of earshot so there was no use in saying 'Hello'. Just before he turned his head to face front again, he squinted for a clearer look at him.

"Oh no, what's that he's waving? Tch, I hope it's not another one of those police posters. It looks about the same size. Bloody hell where is he getting them from?" he exclaimed out loud in the safety of his isolation.

That evening he decided to spoil himself by having another massage from Vanya before a drink and an early night's sleep. He set out to meet Borka the following morning. How the day's events were to unfold concerned him during the taxi ride. The visit being a social one made it unique. It meant both had to amuse and interest each other with more than just the subject of the house build. He struggled to imagine it possible, as he presumed they had nothing in common. He quietly spoke out his thoughts during the journey, assuming the driver had no English. He never gave any reply in Bulgarian or English to Charlie's greeting. So, it made him feel safe to speak his thoughts out loud, knowing they'd remained private. Plus, using the driver as an involuntary confidante, relaxed and helped Charlie make sense of what he was saying. The driver's muted state provided a comfort and gave Charlie the impression he was agreeing with his assessment of Borka.

He mumbled his analysis of Borka. "I think Borka shows himself to be a bit of a rough diamond and his lack of sophistication is more visible than any intelligence. What am I going to do if he appears dressed in a wrestler's outfit and wanting to go a few rounds to work up an appetite for lunch?" He took a quick look at the driver to make sure of no sign he understood him. As expected, the driver appeared expressionless and remained staring at the road.

Charlie continued, "What if Borka wants to box a few rounds with me in the afternoon before eating a whole pig for dinner? Then finally finishing the day off with drinking bottles of Rakia and arm wrestling?" He stopped talking after realising he didn't have powers to anticipate the future with such accuracy. Also, since his forecast of Borka's behaviour was slightly exaggerated – to say the least.

After a little more time rationalising foreboding thoughts, his anxiety lifted and again he spoke, "No, it won't be that bad. Then again, and just in case, I should have bought loads of small mints, put them in a bottle and tell Borka I am on medication. It would provide me an excuse from taking part in any overzealous or health-threatening revelry he might have planned for me!"

At this latter point in his character assassination of Borka, he felt even more comfortable in the company of his silent driver. Charlie raised his voice and even turned his head as though addressing the driver, deciding to further elaborate. He continued, "After all, national pride sometimes becomes a focus in people of different nationalities coming together for a venture. While both are keen to promote an affable manner, so too does a will to promote themselves as good as the other." After staring at the road in silence for another few seconds, he said, "Tch, I should have brought a dartboard. I'm half decent at the game and sure I'd easily beat him. Mm, I wonder do they play darts in Bulgaria? Ah, or Irish dancing would be an impressive display of a talent. Pity I didn't learn it!'.

The taxi approached Borka's house, Charlie thanked and paid the driver. Just as he climbed out the driver leant over, smiled and said in poor English, "Borka good, Irish dancing good, I play darts, London good. Good day." He closed Charlie's door and drove off leaving him outside Borka's house looking frozen faced. It took him five seconds to recover from the shock and said, "Aha, right, shit! I wonder how much of everything before Irish dancing he understood?"

Borka suddenly appeared from his house and exclaimed, "Hallo Charlie, come, I show."

Charlie stared at him with a nervous guilty smile while thinking, "If he heard what I just said about him, he'd probably knock me and my house down!" The two walked around outside for a while with Charlie noticing the huge fire pit for spit roasting. Borka saw him look at it and then pointed while saying, "Next time you come, we eat whole pig."

On hearing that, Charlie thought nervously about how much less than a whole pig did he plan for them to eat today? They went inside and sat on the upstairs balcony. A television set was fixed on the outside wall showing Bulgaria playing in a football game. It helped with conversation as everyone knew something about sport.

Charlie said, "I like boxing." Borka then spoke about Serafim Todorov, who came from the region. He got up from his chair and started shadow boxing around the balcony while speaking. Bulgaria suddenly scored in the football match and Borka's hands shot up in the air from his previous horizontal jabbing. Charlie stole a glance at his watch and wondered how much of the day was remaining, despite knowing he'd only arrived. Borka went back to shadow boxing and from growing confidence tried to do some fancy footwork. It wasn't very impressive, and he tripped on the edge of a floor tile sending him crashing onto his backside.

Charlie, suddenly switching from consternation to a light heartedness, instinctively started to count to ten, as is done by referees in boxing matches. Laughs erupted from both while Charlie looked down at him and waving his arm in time with every number of the count, "One ah, two ah, three ah…" At that very moment all felt so perfect for him. Both were in complete harmony for the first time. Charlie's mental guard was down along with Borka's physical guard from the fall. He instantly knew that Borka's reaction to the comical episode was a sign of him fully accepting Charlie. Though soon his childish way switched to concern. After helping Borka up onto his feet, Borka's rear end had revealed two cracked floor tiles. Charlie frowned while thinking of his own tiling yet to be done. It made him look at the finishing standard of Borka's house and examine it whenever he wasn't present. It wasn't great and reminded him of an adage. One that stated how many builders' houses were in terrible disrepair from them being too busy working on other people's houses.

Borka's future son-in-law _ Kamen – now joined them on the balcony and went to a barbecue in a corner. Charlie's eyes followed him to the BBQ zone and saw a huge amount of meat piled high. He hoped Borka was hungry enough to eat most of it and that he only expected Charlie to eat what he wanted. To be a kind of wingman rather than the leader. Drinking began and conversation too, while Kamen cooked. By eleven pm, Charlie's stomach was so stretched, he thought he'd have to ask someone to cut his trousers off. He couldn't imagine ever being able to undo it. Incredibly, Borka was only warming up at this time, and equally incredible was his suddenly producing a trumpet and raising it to his lips. Pointing it at the forested hills beyond the balcony, he played a melody not dissimilar to a Mexican mariachi heartbreak. It really was impressive and surreal. A nighttime breeze was bending the tall thin trees of the pine forest while carrying Borka's trumpets notes into them.

Just as Kamen and Charlie settled into what they thought would be a nice spell of entertainment, Borka suddenly stopped. Putting down his trumpet and grabbing five record albums, he held them out like a child for Charlie to pick one. Not looking at what he picked, he gave one to Borka, who put it onto the turntable which sat under the TV. Out blared "Please Release Me" by Engelbert Humperdinck. Charlie was again thrown off course with his expectations of Borka's behaviour that evening. Not wanting to miss the unique moment, he joined the two and all three sang "Please Release Me" to the swaying trees beyond.

The night became early morning and Charlie desperately needed to be on his own to somehow try to ease his uncomfortable bloated feeling. Making his excuses, he walked to his room while remembering Borka's earlier invite to Greece the next day. He thought, "Oh God, I'm done in from all the meat, I'll need a week to get over this." He sat in a corner chair for the few remaining hours of darkness, thinking it the safest position to sleep in case he became sick. While attempting to sleep, he thought of Borka's fart when his bum hit the balcony floor. So, to pass the time, he chose to analyse the rights and wrongs of someone farting in the company of others. He knew the bodily function was understandable when impossible to control – as was Borka's that evening. Though, surely not when a fart was voluntary rather than involuntary. This was the case when Borka farted in his office in front of Charlie during their first meeting. It was voluntary because he raised one cheek to release it. Charlie still couldn't sleep.

"Charliee, Charliee, wake up. We go Greece," said Borka while knocking the bedroom door at seven am. Charlie heard him loud and clear, as he had remained awake for almost all the time since entering the room. He had sat upright all night while taking occasional looks at the door, anticipating Borka's knock.

Feeling like a prisoner or hunted man hearing his captor's knock calling him to his fate, he slowly rose to his feet. Staggering from the bedroom to wash himself and greet Borka, he made no attempt to hide his worn-out and tired look. He used it as a pre-emptive measure, to warn Borka of a change of mind about going to Greece with him. Charlie also didn't speak while getting ready and walking to Borka's four-by-four. All this was purposely done to lessen any surprise from Borka regarding his change of mind. The first part of the journey followed the same route for Greece and Ovineshta.

Just before the junction which marked the point where routes to Greece and Ovineshta changed, Borka stopped and looked at Charlie. "You want to go Greece?" he asked.

Charlie looked back apologetically and said, "Sorry, Borka, it's really nice of you to offer, but I'm not up to it and I'll go back to Ovineshta," Being at a desolate junction without any hope of ordering a taxi didn't bother Charlie. He would have walked back to Ovineshta rather than face a hectic day of participating in 'Borkaland' with a near-bursting stomach.

On hearing Charlie politely decline the offer, Borka again surprised him. He got out and waved down a passing vehicle. It was incredible to see such an action for a non-emergency situation. Borka commandeered the driver like bandits would do to a stagecoach in the 'wild west'. After some talking between driver and Borka, he waved Charlie over to the stranger's car. Before getting into it, he gave Borka a longer than usual wave. He felt guilty turning down his invite, though the preoccupation with curing his nausea offset any regret of not going to Greece. He knew that in the morning when feeling better, the Greek trip with Borka would become much more sorely missed.

However, more important was the fact that he hadn't seen the last of Borka. Sitting in the man's car reminded him of his previous taxi and embarrassment. So, he turned to the driver and asked if he knew the man who just stopped him. The driver understood and said, "No." Charlie laid back and closed his eyes in comfort. Knowing that should he – doubtfully – talk in his sleep about Borka, the driver would remain clueless.

Chapter 6

Back in Bonkas and lying on his hotel bed, Charlie waited until his stomach pain eased. By late afternoon, he was back to normal and decided it was time to explore the surrounding region. It was an equally important aspect of his project as the house build. A proverb popped into his head which pleased him as he thought it could be used to support his comparison. Its correct use was to explain something else. However, Charlie was having fun with it because he believed it to be an interchangeable one. He quietly recited it, "While looking at a doughnut, don't focus on the hole." Its original meaning referred to the reasoning that people should focus on what they had and not what they didn't own.. Charlie's new interpretation was the house being the hole and its surrounding area being the doughnut. Both were important and need each other for the product to exist. It wasn't a particularly poetic proverb and sounded too efficient and modern. Many proverbs learnt from his school days were so much more poetic and cryptic. Less obvious but still easy to understand than modern ones. With hands behind his head, he returned his thoughts to choosing what to explore the next day. There were mountain trails and the lakes to see, the Dobrinishte to Septemvri narrow-gauge railway line to travel, also horse riding and even a bear sanctuary. The narrow-gauge railway journey appealed to him the most. Convenient, too, because Dobrinishte was only a short taxi ride from his hotel.

The next morning, he stood for a moment outside Dobrinishte railway station before entering. He wanted to study its architecture and layout. It was refreshingly free of all the infrastructure seen in western cities' stations. There were no complicated gates or turnstiles, or big megaphones for announcements. No garish-coloured signs or paving and hardly any notices to spoil the original look of all before him. The decadence of the place and absence of people made him feel he was the first to rediscover it. Instead of walking through the main door, he went along a short side passage which took him straight onto the platform. He looked down its length bathed in sunlight and at the weeds growing up between the cracks. On the platform stood wooden benches, still firm enough to hold a weary passenger. Their slats had split from the sun and the paint was peeling. He saw only one figure standing motionless further down the platform and walked towards the person for a closer look. As he got closer, he saw a station-master's hat atop a head, with squinting eyes fixed firmly on Charlie. He planned to walk past him and turn around after five paces, in hope that the man would have stopped looking. Charlie turned after the five paces and the man was still looking at him. "Tch, he must be related to that woman who stared at me when the cock flew past my head that time," he said. Turning around again to look along the train track carving its way through the countryside, he saw his train approach. It was old stock, so it didn't embarrass or challenge the station for best looks. Both aging components complimented each other, like two old friends. With the train standing still on the platform, a complete picture was formed of what looked like a quaint working museum.

Charlie climbed aboard and sat down for a wondrous journey over mountains, through tunnels and alongside rivers. He decided to travel as far as Velingrad and return, instead of going all the way to Septemvri and back. Sitting on hard seats for so long had nothing to do with his decision. It was rather that the three-plus hours to Velingrad would provide Charlie with enough supply of gorgeous and unique sights. Narrow-gauge railway lines were few in number around the world and this one carved a route as high as thirteen-hundred metres above sea level. It allowed a daring passenger to touch tunnel walls through open windows while the train passed through barely adequate openings. Then, there were all the huge gorges to view. The train journey reminded him of being told a funny peculiarity for some Bulgarian train drivers. An ex-driver told him trains had a swivel seat for the driver. They were very useful for drivers in sudden need of toilet relief while working. They allowed a driver to swivel on the seat and pee out of the door. While funny to hear, it was also incredible to think of the potential danger to passengers from a driver with a weak bladder. The image of a driver's body facing the door of his compartment, instead of the tracks in front of the train, was a daunting one. Thinking about hearing the story, he wished he had thought of asking about the routine during the freezing winter months. "Is there a chance of the pee freezing and causing problems?" he wondered. He carried on with his increasingly ridiculous train of thought and remembered a rail poster slogan in England from the past. It advertised quicker train journeys and read, 'Slash Your Train Journey'. He knew the word 'slash' was a slang word for urinating and imagined a Bulgarian train driver with good English laughing at the poster. Also, possibly being excused for thinking he would be allowed to 'slash' out of his compartment door if driving a British train.

The return trip to Dobrinishte had an hour remaining, so he continued with his outlandish thoughts while looking at the passing scenery. The following scene played out in Charlie mind. He imagined a Bulgarian train driver with weak kidneys arriving at Ascot Station. He had a sudden urge to relieve himself and had to 'slash' out of his compartment door across the platform as the train slowed to enter the station. The platform was full of recently arrived racecourse goers in all their finery. All were splattered and splashed with urine as it flew from the compartment door at head height. Bouncing off men's top hats and strafing women's dresses, giving them new polka-dot designs. Then comically, everyone on the platform looked up and mistook the spray for light rain as they blamed the sky. The train driver was holding his mouth in disbelief and fear from inevitable blame. Charlie grinned at the absurdity of it as his real train entered Dobrinishte.

Returning his thoughts to reality again, he disembarked and set off for his hotel in Bonkas. Before going off to sleep, he returned to his Ascot scenario because of suddenly recalling a similar, but true incident. It made his own fabricated dream seem not so ridiculous after all. The real-life story was about the opening of a new Wild West Museum. A longhorn bull was strapped hanging from a helicopter and flew to the venue to promote its opening. While it passed over to eventually land, the gathered celebrities and VIPs looked up in amazement. As the bull came closer to the upward-looking visitors, it became nervous and released a shower of urine over all below. Everyone ran for cover through the only set of doors of the venue. Meaning that most were at the mercy of descending bull pee! Clothes were wet, stained, and many rubbed stinging eyes. Anyone who had escaped the golden shower must have been laughing for a week!

Thoughts turned to London the next morning, but one more visit to the house before his flight would be comforting. On arriving, he went straight upstairs to one of the balconies to once more stare at the Pirin Mountains. The breeze felt stronger than any previous visit and made him focus on future maintenance of the house. It was timber-framed and would need careful monitoring for any rot from the elements. With this in mind, he looked at its timber construction and saw how the corner post of the balcony had a few splits. They were larger than he thought acceptable because of it being an important structural timber. Stepping back from the balcony to the bedroom door for another studied look, he heard a sound coming from downstairs. While standing motionless for a few seconds to determine it, Mr 'Evro's' grinning face appeared through the balustrade as he climbed the stairs. Stabbing the floor with his stick in time with each step, he made his way towards Charlie and greeted him. "*Dobar den*."

"*Dobar den*," replied Charlie. Looking out at the balcony and pointing, Charlie continued, "Look, splits in the timber post, I must raise this concern with Borka." Mr Evro could only look back at him. Charlie knew he didn't understand but telling him made him feel his problem was shared and gave him comfort. He wanted to say it again, so with arm raised and finger pointing at the post he said, "Look, split in post, split!"

"Aaargh," replied Mr Evro. Charlie was amazed by his sound of recognition at what he just said, and the man replied, "*Neh, Gotzeh Delchev*." Charlie's face creased with confusion. He knew Gotzeh Delchev was a town further south near the Greek border, but wondered why he said it. "*Neh split, Gotzeh Delchev dah*," said the man again. Then the reason for his response dawned on him and thought, "He thinks I'm pointing down the valley, instead of the post. How I'm saying the Croatian city of Split is there."

He continued, "Oh no, I can see where this conversation is going." Not bothering to correct the confusion, he only smiled at Mr Evro and said, "*Dah*," and continued to survey the house for any more snags. Mr Evro then made a gesture to the en-suite toilet. "Oh no, what is he doing now, he doesn't want to go to the toilet, does he?" said Charlie. Going over to the toilet and bending his legs, as though to sit down on it, Charlie said, "*Neh, neh voda.* There is no plumbing or water, *neh voda.*"

Mr Evro laughed and said, "*Neh neh*," while wagging a finger and pointing in the direction of his own house. After further thought, Charlie realised that his interest in the toilet suite was because it matched his own one. He relaxed from the slightly anxious moment and the two laughed. A mutual feeling of understanding each other was realised on something other than a 'hello' or 'goodbye'. Charlie returned to surveying the house and making mental notes of issues needing attention, with Mr 'Evro' following him. The previous scene with the toilet made him return and refocus on it. On closer inspection, it looked dated and was probably chosen by Borka to save money. It went on the list of things to highlight.

The two eventually descended the stairs to leave and lock up. Both gave each other hearty 'goodbyes' until their next meeting. Charlie had taken a quick look at Mr Evro's pockets to see if any posters were visible. He couldn't see any and said, "Phew, thank God for that. Hopefully he's got tired of that obsession." He decided to walk down to the square then call a taxi. There was a slight fall, making it easier on the legs and less effort than walking up to the house. For fun, he kicked any stray olives which had fallen from the many olive trees lining the streets. The sun was on his back, and he felt happy. Nearing the square, he took his phone and called a taxi to take him back to his hotel. He needed to prepare for his journey back to London.

He decided to stay overnight in Sofia at the Jasmine Hotel. It was highly recommended to him for a nice experience. Once again, he disembarked a bus at Ovcha Kupel Station. He eagerly looked at taxi drivers making sure he didn't pick the same one as before. He thought lightening rarely struck the same place twice, and he presumed he'd have a hassle-free lift to Hotel Jasmine. Wrong! Charlie's intuition let him down again because he picked another inadequate driver. After getting into the cab, he asked for Jasmine Hotel. The driver didn't look at him and just said, "Da." After what seemed a long time, the driver stopped and looked at a map. Obviously, he was lost, and Charlie's enquiring was of no use as the driver couldn't speak English.

"Not again, what is it with me and taxi drivers?" he mumbled. After a little while the driver moved on and Charlie hoped to see a hotel reception desk soon. Another twenty minutes passed, and Charlie saw Princess Hotel come into view. "Oh no, he's not going to pull in there – is he? He is!" Charlie exclaimed. Turning to the driver he said, "Are you related to my previous driver at Ovcha Kupel? This is not Jasmine Hotel, look it says in big letters 'Princess Hotel'. Why did you bring me here," he desperately asked. The driver sensed his frustration and gave an equally desperate reply with a shrug of his shoulders. That shrug of his shoulders was a sign Charlie wouldn't be getting to Jasmine Hotel anytime soon – if at all. After more talking and both not understanding the other, the driver put one finger in the air as though suddenly realising a solution. He drove off and Charlie relaxed. The driver's pointed finger had signalled inspired thought to his passenger in reaching their destination. Another fifteen minutes passed, and Charlie felt more foreboding. Buildings had become sparse and he felt they were entering the suburbs, or further. In the near distance appeared a tall building, it was isolated and Charlie squinted to see any sign reading Jasmine Hotel. As they drew nearer and the building became clearer, Charlie exclaimed, "Ah no, I don't believe this. What are you doing? That's a signal tower, why are you taking me to the airport?" The driver stopped outside arrivals and gave another shrug of his shoulders. Charlie spontaneously decided not to pay him and got out to go inside the airport. He found an English-speaking worker who called him a suitable taxi driver. It arrived and Charlie got in, the previous driver was still parked. Then, the saga turned to farce because the new driver was very old and his right to possess a licence was questionable. Charlie was asking him to speed up because the previous driver was following them for his fare. After a couple of minutes, he asked his driver to stop, got out and paid the previous cab. Charlie had felt his decision not to pay was too harsh – despite the terrible service. He paid what he thought was a fare portion of his fare. After another night's sleep he went for his flight to London the following afternoon.

Next day, he parked across the road from the job, he decided to stay in his car to watch Ms Belcher. She was making repeat trips to her rubbish bin out in the front. He eventually got out and walked over, lifting the lid and looking inside before passing by. Inside were mirrors and lots of wine bottles. She made one more trip to it, dropping in another mirror and ignoring him.

"Morning to you, too, Ms Belcher," said Charlie in a slightly sarcastic tone.

Entering the house, he saw Nelly at the top of the stairs looking down at him. She pointed an index finger towards her temple while mouthing, "She loco."

He went straight to the loft and heard Andy and Tagaby in heated debate. "You should get the Historical Re-enactment Society to play out your last date with a woman. It's been so long you must have forgotten what it was like – ha," said Tagaby.

"Well, at least I didn't get barred from my own home when I did have a girlfriend – ha to you, too," Andy replied.

"Okay, boys, how's things? Mm, loft looking good," interrupted Charlie. The first fixing of the electrics and plumbing were nearly complete and things seemed in order. "I better go down and see Ms Belcher," he said. Nelly was waiting for him at the bottom of the ladder and keen to speak with him. "What is it, Nelly? Oh, before I forget, here's your bottle of Rakia," he said.

"Ah, brilliant, and I forgot I asked you to bring one, thanks Charlie. Listen, I must tell you, she had the house exorcised!" she replied.

"No way, seriously?"

She laughed while looking to check Ms Belcher and Dick were out of earshot and said, "Let me explain. It was arranged two days ago. She went along with my suggestion of getting a Bulgarian priest to carry it out. The idea was to avoid any gossip from a local priest doing it – remember?" she asked.

With eyes like saucers and in anticipation, Charlie asked "Okay, so how did it go?"

"Oh brilliant, I made £100," she replied.

"What, how come?" he asked.

"I got a friend of mine to dress up as an Orthodox priest and do the ceremony. I told Ms Belcher it would cost £200. You know, for his church fund, and we split the money!" she replied.

"You're mad," he exclaimed.

"Charlie, she treats me like a dog sometimes and she pays terrible wages. Anyway, it was so cool, he came in plain clothes and changed in the front room, but he had trouble sticking the big beard on. He thought having a big beard would make him look more genuine, like the priests you see in films," she said.

"This is mad. What about your friend, what does he really do?" he asked.

"Oh, he's a musician friend from my hometown and plays here in a pub band. He thought he'd have some fun with Ms Belcher and made her kiss his hand, saying it was traditional in Bulgaria. I think he might have been a bit high on drugs from the previous night, too, and did well to keep up the act. He chanted a song as he walked around the house with an incense vessel," she enthusiastically recalled.

"Is that how an exorcism is done?" he asked.

"I don't know. Neither does he, I think. He just improvised. He told me afterwards that he was chanting a pop song about two lovers – ha ha. It was all in Bulgarian, so she didn't know. Ah, so funny I had to leave the house so I could laugh," she said.

"I can't believe this happened. You're mental, Nelly. What about the incense burner? I mean, what was in it? Dope, I guess? No?" he asked.

"Ha, no, he used something he pulled from a park on the way here, but the funniest is to come. He must've been high because I wouldn't have said what he did to Ms Belcher," she said.

"Oh no, said what?" enquired Charlie.

"He said to Ms Belcher that he'd have to return to do another exorcism because the loft wasn't finished. Oh, it was so clever because we can make some more money," she said proudly. Switching to a serious face, she continued, "Oh there's more, too."

Charlie had switched off listening by this stage of the story and while looking out of a window said, "God, this is unbelievable."

Nelly then said while grinning mischievously, "There's one more thing."

"Crikey, there's more?" exclaimed Charlie.

"Yes, before my friend left, he asked for a bottle of wine for the church. Dick then appeared from somewhere and gave him two bottles," she said.

"Ah, lucky friend, I supposed he's drunk them already," said Charlie mockingly.

Not realising his jesting, she replied, "Probably, but it could have gone all wrong at the last moment."

"Oh why?" he asked.

"Dick asked where was his church located. My friend was quick to reply so not to create any suspicion from a hesitation," she explained.

"Okay, well, at least he wasn't found out, or else you could be talking to the boys in blue," said Charlie.

"What's that?" she asked.

"Ah forget it, it's the police, anyway. What address did he give for the church?" enquired Charlie.

"Oh, I think I heard him give some numbers like a post code or something. I'm sure it was W1D5BR," she said.

"Okay, best check on the phone to see if it exists, in case Dick or Sue decides to visit," he said. Taking his phone in hand and searching the post code, Charlie's face went white and said, "Oh my God, what have you done Nelly? That post code is Horse Guards Parade."

"What's that, a racetrack or something?" she exclaimed.

"No, no, you idiot, it's our Queen's parade ground, near Downing Street, you know, where the Prime Minister lives!" Both stared at each other, Nelly's eyes now as big as Charlie's from shock "Listen, Nelly, for your sake, I hope Dick has a sense of humour. If he decides to visit that post code on a particular day and be greeted by a load of horses and an army band instead of a priest, you're both for the 'high jump'," he said.

Looking away from Nelly he continued, "I better go downstairs and report to her." Turning around for one more look at her, he said, "And don't ask me what I meant by 'high jump'. You may soon find out. See you in a bit."

Approaching Ms Belcher on the ground floor, he was greeted with, "I've thrown some mirrors in the bin and stored the expensive ones."

That was all she said, and Charlie replied, "Okay, fine, how are you anyway? I heard about the exorcism. So, you're ghost-free now – if there was one!"

"Oh yes, there's a young one after me all right, ooh yes. It's a dark force from the past. Don't think it was a burglar, after all," she said, staring out of the kitchen window.

"Okay, but how did the exorcism go?"

Her mood changed on hearing the question and spun round like a whirling dervish. Her mouth and eyes wide open, she enthusiastically replied, "Oh, it was wonderful, the priest had a fancy frock, big beard and hat. He waved loads of smelly incense around the rooms, and I kissed his hand!" Charlie wondered was it his guitar strumming hand she kissed. She continued and spat out the following words, "Anyway, mustn't hold you up," while bouncing on her toes and tapping her hands together in a praying position. Charlie saw her crescendo of madness, possibly to peak and manifest itself in some strange outburst soon.

Going back upstairs, he passed Dick coming out of the bedroom with a glass of wine and book. The book was upside down and gave away the truth he was just drinking. His breath smelt of alcohol most of the day and he was an alcoholic. He was unintentionally growing a beard and his glasses were halfway down his nose. "Ah, beards are all the fashion now since the priest's visit?" Charlie joked.

"I must use the shed from now onwards, but it's too cold. That's why I now have a beard growing," he replied.

Charlie frowned and carried the cryptic reply with him to the loft. He'd repeat it to the others in hope of an answer to its meaning. "What did he mean by, 'Shed too cold and that's why I have a beard'?" he asked.

"I saw him go outside one day to the shed with a towel and shaving gear. Whatever that was about," said Andy.

"Nelly told me the priest advised Ms Belcher to get rid of the mirrors after the exorcism – even the bathroom one. Something to do with ghosts being attracted to them," said Tagaby.

"I see, weird. So, the shed is the only place he is allowed to shave with a mirror. Then because it's too cold, he's decided to grow a beard. God, I hope we get paid at the end of this job. It's getting crazier by the day here," Charlie concluded.

Dick's maturing beard came to the rescue in an earlier exchange between himself and wife Sue over his drinking. He had used to dispose of his many empty wine bottles in Charlie's skip outside, to disguise his addiction from her. Tagaby took them out to save until he had a large number gathered.

Then he put them into the wheelie bin one day to see for any reaction from Sue. There was! On finding the bottles she went on the attack. "What the bloody hell is that out there?" she shouted at Dick while pointing a finger at the wheelie bin. The bottles were pushing the lid open from there being so many. She continued, "My God, I know I like a drink, but I never knew you could drink for the two of us."

Dick remained impressively calm during her verbal attack. His nervous system was suitably relaxed from bathing in half a bottle of something he had just drunk. "What do you mean? Those clarets aren't mine, they must be the workers," he feebly replied.

"Ha, how come you know the bottles are clarets if they're not yours?" she retorted with scary eyes.

He couldn't answer her, so tried to mitigate her attack by exclaiming, "Anyway, I'm saving a fortune on not being able to use razors to shave because of your stupid ban on mirrors." He made a tactical retreat to his study while she considered his retort.

Deciding to leave the house and make a call to Borka from home, Charlie met Nelly in the hall on leaving. "Nelly, what's all this about the mirrors?" he asked.

"Oh, I forgot to tell you, my friend made up something about mirrors attracting ghosts. He advised her to get rid of them and offered to take them away. He'll make good money reselling them," she said.

"Tch, I don't believe you two. Where do you get off? While he was at it, why didn't he suggest Ming vases are a big attraction for ghosts, too? There's one in the front room and worth more money than all the mirrors put together," he replied sarcastically.

Nelly, looking embarrassed, said "Sorry."

Charlie replied, "I must go and make a call, bye for now."

Getting in touch with Borka was difficult because of three things. He was often on the road visiting projects and his voice message mailbox was always full. Emailing wasn't ideal because of constant misinterpretations. Finally, whenever his calls were answered, they were done so by his secretary. Fruitless replies would come from her, telling Charlie to phone Borka's son-in-law requesting that he send a message to Borka. Kamen would answer, but Charlie always wondered if his messages were passed on. Also, he knew that any messages from a second party often lost any importance or urgency. Plus, there were unsuitable delays in replies from Borka to any messages received. His concerns about some of the build quality needed Borka's urgent attention. The sooner the better too, before further work commenced. The calls to Borka continued until he made contact. In the meantime, he bought materials for the loft job and paid site visits. A pleasant surprise was one of hearing Nelly later convincing her 'priest' friend not to sell the mirrors.

Finally, Borka answered his phone. "Hallo Charliee how is you?" he asked.

"Hello Borka, hope you're well. It's difficult getting hold of you, I need to talk about the house. Some things need attention, there are problems," he replied. The call was difficult because of background noise on Borka's end.

"Problem? Come show, I come see with you. When you come?" he asked

"Okay, I'll fly as soon as I can and let you know?" replied Charlie.

He organised another flight and was back in Bulgaria. Deciding to stay in Ovineshta this time, he picked Hotel Rumyana. It had a stream running outside and high trees along its bank, their branches nearly stretching to the hotel's balconies. It was traditional in appearance, located in a pleasant setting and that was why he chose it. Arriving at the check-in desk, he experienced his first surprise of the day. The man signing him in was the driver of the car on that scary journey around Ovineshta. He gave Charlie a knowing smile and said, "Hello." He made no further reference to that day in the car, or surprise at seeing him again. Charlie replied in similar fashion and went to his room. He didn't disparage him for his reluctance to communicate further, rather taking it as him being busy. Besides, he had plenty of time later to connect with him properly.

The meeting with Borka in the late afternoon was uppermost in Charlie's mind. There wasn't much of the summer left. The nights had turned colder, and the days were shortening. The appointment was for five pm and he strolled up to the house on time. He waited, waited and waited, but no sign of Borka. He knew he had to drive from Pazetahra, which was over one hundred kilometres away, so he factored in potential delays over such a distance. Standing there alone in a dark, empty, cold house, focused his mind deeper on the reason for his Bulgarian project. Five pm had become nine pm, and there was still no sign of Borka.

Staring out of a window towards Mr 'Evro's' property in the distance, he spotted a small window light and mumbled, "I bet he's warm now. Maybe sitting by an open fire and counting all the police posters of me he's gathered." He prolonged the mock scene to distract himself from the cold. "I should go over there and knock on his door, give him a surprise. He's nice and sure he'd offer me a seat. Maybe his wife would sing again. I could sneak around and look for any posters and take them. I can see those things popping up somewhere again and really embarrassing me."

Thoughts of doubt about his Bulgarian venture then took control of his mind, to perplex Charlie, and again, he mumbled, "What am I doing here? Have I made a mistake doing this build? I'm single, so no need for this house." He feared his 'ship of thoughts' was listing and looked for something to get it on an even keel. He reminded himself of the reason for the project. "Mind, this house was to satisfy my desire to build something, so it fulfilled the professional side of life. Mm, but a house must be filled afterwards. Ah who knows, maybe I'll meet someone," he told himself. Then struck with an inspired thought, he continued, "I know, I'll sell it and do it again, but build a log house next time. I've noticed one go up not too far away and they're lovely." He stopped mumbling and gave his mind a rest. He became silent to just simply stare out of the window into the distance.

About fifteen seconds later, a beam of light suddenly shot across the wall in front of him. Turning around to look out of another window, he saw the headlights of a vehicle approaching his house. Still not being able to see anything other than headlamps, he watched them grow bigger as they came closer. The car stopped a short distance away and the sound of a door being opened, then slammed closed was heard. Charlie fumbled in the dark for the handle of a door to open and investigate.

Ten – barely audible – footsteps later, Borka's head appeared out of the darkness. "Hallo Charliee," he said.

There was a smell of drink from him and Charlie wasn't impressed. It was ten pm, dark, he was five hours late and had very little chance of seeing anything properly. Plus, depending how much Borka had drunk, all or some of the issues to be discussed might be forgotten by him later. Charlie's greeting was less than enthusiastic. Nevertheless, and despite the situation the two were in, some resolution to complaints might be gained. He saw a torch light in his hand, which made him think his late arrival was planned. Charlie surmised that a dark house was more beneficial for Borka, in that highlighting unsatisfactory work could be a problem for Charlie. Borka couldn't get the torch to work. At one point, Charlie stepped forward in the pitch dark and walked into something hard and immovable. Thinking it was a wall or edge of a door, he stepped back to realise it was Borka. Borka acted as though he didn't feel anything and remained with head bent fiddling with his torch.

"Crikey, this guy is like a brick outhouse," thought Charlie. Immediately revising his approach to Borka, he thought, "I better take him easy and not get too assertive. He's got beer in him, hard as steel and there's just the two of us here in dark isolation. Mind you, should he lose his cool, it'd be difficult for him to hit me in the dark. Plus, the booze wouldn't help his aim." Quickly rationalising the situation, he thought, "No, don't be silly, just be nice to him and forget any strong criticism or bossing during his visit."

Borka finally got his torch lit and they proceeded with the survey of snags. As Charlie anticipated, the visit was not as satisfactory as he hoped. They staggered and tripped around the house while the torch beam flew in all directions. Charlie was at least able to physically tell him about his concerns. While reading off his mental list to him, he couldn't help thinking it went in one of Borka's ears and straight out the other. He stated the old plumbing suites were not satisfactory, and his concerns about the wide split in a balcony post, the remaining tiling, stone cladding and more.

Borka was compliant and listened to Charlie without interruption and happily saying, "Yes," to everything. He swayed and looked through sleepy eyes surrounded by a smell of drink. A waft of it brushed Charlie's nostrils with his every "yes." Normally he would be grateful and thankful for such a positive response. However, he was unconvinced that corrections would be made until he saw them on his next visit. The meeting marked a change in attitudes and Charlie sensed the honeymoon period with him could well be over.

Chapter 7

Having returned to his room, he stood looking out of the window, thinking what to do for the next day. The train journey during his previous visit came to mind, making him decide on another outing. He chose the Belitsa Bear Sanctuary roughly thirty to forty kilometres away. Petar was on the desk again in the morning and called a taxi for Charlie's trip. Just as he went to leave, he called and said with a smile, "Come in bar for drink evening."

"Ah great, thanks, I will, ciao," replied Charlie. Those few words offset miserable thoughts of his disappointment with Borka the previous night. Also, he felt it made up for the poor welcome on his arrival.

Belitsa Bear Sanctuary was a huge estate of around one-hundred-and-twenty-thousand square metres – about thirty acres. Charlie tried to picture the size by dividing it by his own plot. "Phew, well over two hundred times my plot," he thought. He knew about the past infamous practice of the dancing bears of east Europe. The sanctuary was a home for those fortunate to have been freed. A guide took him and his group of tourists around the complex while explaining the aim of the charity. Then at the end, visitors were ushered into a room to watch a captured video tape showing barbaric treatment of a dancing bear. A gruesome history for some bears, but now many were in this happy and safe environment. One bear's experience took prominence in Charlie's mind. It had been plied with so much alcoholic drink during its street dancing days, it nearly went blind. As a result, staff at the sanctuary had to dig the bear's lair. Charlie felt guilty when a vision of Borka popped into his head on the journey back to his hotel. It wasn't because of his recent house visit, but rather for his similarity to an upright bear. Minus a metre or two in height – of course!

After a rest and freshening up, he went to the ground floor restaurant for a meal at seven pm. It looked as he expected and appealed to him. It was a typical *mehana,* looking cosy and homely from its layout. Solid dark brown wooden furniture contrasted with the red and white tablecloths. Flames danced in the open fire while other flames were at work heating pots in a clay oven. He sat down and took hold of a menu to study.

The first thing he read was 'wolf's bits.' "God, what's that? I think I'll give that a miss. It's all bears and wolves so far today," he mused. He ordered Chomlek, a lovely Balkan stew cooked in a wood fired oven and a Zagorka beer to drink with it. Looking up at a door, he saw a beast's claw attached to it, acting as a coat hanger. "Maybe customers who don't pay their bills have a hand cut off and used as a coat hanger," he jested. Just as he was finishing his meal, Petar walked in with two men. Charlie recognised the other two as being those men in the car with

Petar on that nerve-racking car ride. He looked for recognition from them. They did by smiling while giving him a quick wave. Petar produced a folded sheet of paper, which he unfolded and lay on the table. All three looked down to study it. Some time later, while Charlie was staring across at them, his line of vision was interrupted. It was by a woman suddenly appearing at his table. "Hello, I'm Rumyana, Petar's wife. How are you?" she asked.

"Hello, I'm Charlie and I'm fine, thank you, I've just had a lovely meal," he replied.

"Thank you, and you're welcome. You are known already by many here, as the Englishman who is building a house. Yet we haven't spoken with you," she said.

"Yes, this is my fifth visit and I must appear like some mystery character. I've been staying in Bonkas for my last trips and now feel guilty for not having stayed here," he explained while smiling.

"Ah, that's okay. Anyway, enjoy your evening," she said.

While watching her walk away and in admiration of her spoken English, two women had sat down, one either side of him. While refocusing on his beer, a third woman then came to join his table and sat opposite Charlie. The situation reminded him of a school experiment showing an isolated magnet slowly attracting iron fillings. From being alone, Charlie was suddenly surrounded by three women. The two either side of him were elderly and the one in front very attractive and possibly late thirties in age. They all knew each other and spoke in Bulgarian while the one next to Charlie knitted. He gave polite smiles whenever catching their eyes and it felt homely being surrounded by the sound of clicking needles, busy talk and a blazing fire. It gave him a sense of belonging. Then to Charlie's surprise, one of the women broke her conversation with the other two. It was the attractive one sitting opposite and she spoke in English, saying, "Hello, how are you? You are not from here?"

Again, Charlie was impressed with her clear English pronunciation and replied, "No, I'm just visiting."

"Is it for a holiday?" she enquired.

"Well, actually no, I'm building a house at the top of town," he explained.

"Where are you from?" she enquired further.

"London," he replied. Her interviewing style of questioning slightly tainted the homely feel for Charlie at that moment. He wondered how the rest of the conversation would go.

"So, you are from London and building a house here," she said rhetorically. Charlie couldn't fathom her mindset on him, as she gave no sign of warmth or specific intention from her questioning. She only asked short probing questions. She continued, "My name is Magdalena. So, will you marry a Bulgarian woman and live here in your house. Or maybe you have wife or girlfriend in London?" she asked.

"Actually, no, no girlfriend or wife. Oh, by the way, I'm Charlie," he replied.

The lacking in warmth from her up to that point suddenly changed. It wouldn't just be the open fire giving off heat from now on. She sat back in her chair draping her shapely legs out in front and in full view of Charlie. She continued but in a provocative tone, "You know, we Bulgarian women know how to love."

Charlie knew this because there were seven million plus people in the country and that didn't happen without love. She said the word 'love' for longer than normal which also made her even more attractive to Charlie. The statement had more warmth to it than her frosty open questioning. Thinking about her statement more seriously, he concluded she had designs on him. Before replying, he carefully chose what to say and replied politely while changing the subject. "I believe you, so what do you do for a living?" he asked.

"I'm a teacher. We work hard. I like to arrive in school at seven am and prepare for the day," she replied. Charlie thought he only had the toothpaste washed from his mouth by seven am. She explained her work with passion that made it sound as though it was a declaration of love. So much so that she made teaching sound sexy. He admired her work ethic and while being impressed, he thought it a little obsessive, too. Despite being a very attractive woman, he considered she might be a task master and very demanding. Of course, he could be wrong, and it was only a first impression. Besides, at that moment, her physical attractiveness offset any concerns about her temperament. She wore a tight jumper and jeans showing a great figure.

Long curly black hair hung down the sides of her soft-skinned face. Rosy lips and big dark eyes competed for attention. Her thick-framed glasses couldn't hide her sexuality – only heightened it. "Oh, teachers are always admired, and you must like children," he replied.

Her look became a more provocative stare and her voice dropped again when replying, "Yes, and a big family is nice. Bulgarian women are the best," stressing the 'best'.

Charlie would normally be dubious of women with deep voices but not Magdalena. She was definitely a woman. He also wondered if she had wolf's bits earlier for dinner and were possibly an aphrodisiac. He couldn't help thinking something made her aroused making him feel like a prey. Looking at her and thinking of the wolf's bits, he pictured her with head arched backwards and howling like a wolf while making love. Also, he wondered would she have spoken so provocatively had the other women understood English.

During the small break in conversation, Charlie wondered what was wrong with a man heard yelping on the other side of the restaurant. It was very annoying and regularly punctured their conversation. Charlie mentioned it to Magdalena who turned to look and reported knowing the man. "Ah, he has a habit of biting the inside of his mouth while eating and he shouts because it hurts. The doctor told him, as we age, our muscles relax. That's why he accidentally bites the inside of his mouth. He has a little lack of control around that area," she said.

"Ah interesting. I suppose how much you bite yourself depends on how hungry you are – ha!" said Charlie, hoping Magdalena would get the feeble joke and hopefully a laugh.

He wasn't to know because she replied, "Yes but you know, Bulgarian women's lips are always strong. Full and ready to do what they must do." She paired the reply with a provocative stare over the top of her glasses. Charlie welcomed it much more than any laugh. He looked back at her wondering what exactly did she mean!

He moved his gaze from Magdalena for a moment and saw a pair of thick wool socks on the edge of the table. "Where did they come from?" he thought surprisingly. The woman sewing seemed to pick up speed and knit much faster since first sitting down. It was as though she became aroused from Magdalena's talk and knitting much quicker as a result. That was despite not understanding the English being spoken. Charlie was sure he saw steam coming from her needles, but it was smoke from the fire in the distance. He turned towards the woman on the other side of him and saw another pair of socks on that side of the table. She gave a knowing smile while sliding the socks closer to him and wished he knew what she was thinking. The evening was an unusual one from flirting in the front and gifts from the side. He switched focus and relaxed his gaze on Petar and company across the room. They were already smiling at him, and it made Charlie think a possible conspiracy was playing out. Possibly one of a matchmaking night and he was the match. He hated the thought of any form of entrapment, but looking across at lovely Magdalena made it an exception. If it was true, he was happy to play along and kept an open mind to any outcome.

Feeling happy from the thought of solving the riddle of the evening, he scanned the room for an update of who was there. He saw it had filled up and looked over to the entrance area. Immediately, his heart sped up from seeing Mr 'Evro' standing there. Grinning and looking towards him, he waved his stick in the air nearly knocking a lantern hanging from the ceiling. Charlie hoped no one knew him so he wouldn't stay long. He dreaded the thought of him pulling out a police poster in front of everyone. He was wrong and the complete opposite happened. Nearly everyone in the restaurant knew him and gave hearty welcomes and waves. Even Magdalena gave a little wave. Charlie's heart was beating as fast as the knitting needles next to him were clicking! He lowered his head while bringing a hand up to stroke his forehead as though in sudden thought as to what would happen next.

Mr 'Evro' appeared larger and larger as he approached his table. Magdalena put an affectionate hand on his shoulder and said, "This is my father." Charlie was stunned by the announcement and just managed to keep his jaw from dropping. The posters came straight to mind and as anticipated, Mr 'Evro' produced one and put it down on the table. He winked at Charlie, gave a little laugh and walked away to another table. "Ah what's this? It's a picture of you, Charlie," Magdalena exclaimed.

"No, let me explain," he quickly replied.

Studying it further she exclaimed, "Oh, it's a police notice. You stole a taxi and you come in here acting innocent."

"No, I didn't, ask your mayoress. She'll explain the truth how I was mistaken for the criminal. I had a living nightmare the time of my first visit and hunted by people here thinking I did it. What would I be doing sitting here if I stole the car?" he pleaded. Charlie gave Mr 'Evro' a stern look of disapproval and received a bigger smile in return.

After a further look at the poster and a pause, she said, "Okay, I believe you for now, but will check with Miss Evdokiya tomorrow,"

"Do, do, I'm telling the truth," he replied. It was late by this time and the change in mood created an awkwardness, prompting an end to the evening. Charlie offered to show his house to Magdalena to offset any disparaging thoughts she might have of him. Her enthusiasm for him quickly returned on hearing his invite and they exchanged numbers. She gave him a hearty goodbye followed with a little wave and big smile. Charlie slept well.

He woke up the next morning and his first thought was one of feeling wanted. Such was the impression given by Magdalena and others in the restaurant. Replaying thoughts of that previous evening would be enough to keep him happy and occupied for the day. He decided to go to Bonkas in the afternoon and do no more than walk around. Strolling aimlessly around a town's streets would be a welcome change from purposely going to buy something. Random looking allowed eyes to discover so many things often otherwise unnoticed. All sorts of cow bells were hanging in one souvenir shop, and he instantly decided to buy one. "Mm, I can hang that small one on my garden tree and it'll chime in the breeze. Ah, I'll get that heavier cow bell too and put it somewhere," he muttered.

He left the shop and continued strolling until he heard his name being called. He turned around to see Vanya smile and call again. Charlie had received a few massages from her when he stayed in Bonkas. He used the same hotel and she ran its spa room. Unfortunately, her English was nearly non-existent. Despite that, an instant aura was created between them on the first meeting and a friendship developed.

"Hallo Charlie," she said.

"Hello Vanya, you're looking *dobre*," said Charlie while holding his arms outstretched and aimed towards her body.

"Ah, *blagodaryah* Charlie, Charlie no massage," she replied while shrugging her shoulders and frowning.

"Sorry, *Neh*, I stay Ovineshta this time, *neh* here, Ovineshta for house, ah, what is the word? *Kushta, kushta*," he desperately explained. She filled in the meaning between the words Ovineshta and *kushta* to understand his explanation. She was further helped by remembering his previous mention of the house.

Tourists staying in hotels were often curiosities for staff members. They liked to know where they came from and any background information was often of interest. When Charlie had first stayed and booked massages with Vanya, the two seemed to connect and relax in each other's company immediately. After probing him about his visit on their first meeting, he explained he was from London and all about his house building plan. He realised later that a foreigner coming to build in Bulgaria could easily create misleading imagery in some people's minds. Some would understand it as being an innocent venture, hobby or passionate project by the person. Though others might understand it as something done by idle rich with nothing better to do with their time and money. Charlie hoped she thought the former, as he was no idle rich man with money or time to burn.

After a few more attempts at communicating, they simultaneously suggested having a coffee and laughed at their suggestions coinciding. Vanya showed the way to a nice open yard in front of a *mehana* where both sat down. Charlie took out his new cow bell and jokingly rang it to call a waiter. Both laughed again, so too did the waiter whose attention was drawn by the sound of the bell. The coffees arrived and they whiled away the time with silent looks, attempts at communicating, mimicking and laughing. When the coffees were halfway down their cups, Vanya gave Charlie a concentrated stare for three seconds, then leant down to her handbag to take out her phone and show a picture of an apartment. She held the phone camera in front of him, eager for him to look. "Ah nice, yours?" he asked.

"*Da*," she replied while not understanding but nodding. "Where, Bonkas?" he continued asking.

"*Da*," she said and nodded again. While both looked at the camera she asked "Massage, massage good?" while pointing to the picture. Charlie looked up for a second, thought he had nothing else to do and agreed. He never knew where she lived and assumed this was her apartment. He thought she decided to use the chance meeting to make some earnings from a treatment. Normally he'd be surprised at being offered to go to the home of a practitioner he'd only recently known. Then after further analysis, he knew they had enough mutual trust for her to trust herself with the offer. They finished their coffee and walked off to the apartment. Charlie appreciated the opportunity for an impromptu massage, especially as he was not staying in Bonkas this time.

They climbed to the second floor and Vanya opened the door. Charlie gave a cursory look around the open lounge and immediately praised it for the sake of politeness. He saw no signs of personal items or pictures and noticed how spotlessly clean it looked. The minimal, uncluttered look appealed to him. He wasn't surprised with the cleanliness, as that was to be expected because of her profession. Plus, he guessed she might have just moved in. That might also have explained the lack of personal items. Her enthusiasm for the apartment was very evident and it was the final piece to convince him she had just moved in. She spun around while standing still. Arms were stretched up and legs crossed, like someone in a television lifestyle advert. He was happy for her and watched her move to the balcony. While looking at her for a moment leaning on it in a dreamy mode, he called, "Vanya." She turned and saw Charlie gesturing a massage action with his hands and pointing to a door. She understood and enthusiastically pointed a finger to the closed door. "Okay, I go get ready?" he asked while still pointing to the door.

"*Da*," she replied on seeing his pointing finger. She was admiring the square below while Charlie entered the room and prepared to undress. He looked around and saw no massage table. Despite it, he started to undress while assuming the treatment room must be the other room. Remaining in his shorts, he folded his clothes and opened the door.

Panic immediately struck Charlie as the door opened. For he now saw a man standing in the lounge! Such was the shock that he was overcome by a sudden weakness. Vision played havoc and his heart sped up along with a sweat. He moved his focus across to Vanya. Her mouth and eyes wide open from seeing a near naked Charlie. Strangely, Charlie's thoughts suddenly switched to his stomach. It wasn't fat but neither was it a 'six pack', though despite it, he decided to suck it in while standing by the open door. Looking back at the man, he saw a face corrugated from frowning and – like Vanya's – it stared back at his nearly naked body.

"Jesus, what's this?" exclaimed Charlie, before shutting himself inside the room without waiting for a reply. He locked the door and stood back from it. "Crikey, is he the husband or what?" he mumbled. Still in panic, he looked out of the window for an escape, quickly forgetting it on seeing he was two floors up. He grabbed his clothes and put them on the quickest he ever had to that date. Just as he was pulling up his jeans, he heard the man's voice on the other side of the door say, "Excuse me, sir, please put your clothes on and come out,"

"Too right I will and they're already on," he replied. Stepping out of the room Charlie saw Vanya covering her open mouth with one hand. The man introduced himself as an estate agent which reduced Charlie's fear. He immediately realised that a huge misunderstanding had just occurred between all present in the room. Surprising too, was seeing Vanya's initial shock being only a mock one for the agent. For she was now standing behind him, out of eyeshot, eyes closed and nearly falling from silent laughter. The estate agent speaking both languages made it possible for quick explanations.

Charlie explained how he thought Vanya owned the flat and offered him a massage. Vanya recomposed herself and stepped back into the agent's view. She explained to him how she brought Charlie to the flat hoping he would help purchase it for her massage business. The agent's response on hearing the unique mishap was to laugh like Vanya, but loudly.

Charlie was completely shocked by the agent's change of mood. He desperately wanted to know what Vanya told him. He gave a confused look at the agent prompting him to explain. He did and Charlie's blushes disappeared while making a sigh of relief. All three stood in a triangle smiling and laughing at the harmless misunderstanding. They felt no harm was done as they all saw the humour in it. It was enough to offset any sense of time having been wasted. Charlie and Vanya said goodbye to the agent. He was still smiling and shaking his head from residual thought of what just happened. Vanya eagerly suggested another coffee to prolong the fun of what happened. Though after agreeing, Charlie tempered the mood for a moment by rebuking her deceitful act of thinking he would help purchase an apartment. He knew she didn't understand what he said, but he needed to satisfy himself by saying it. They parted after another hour, and he was soon back in Ovineshta.

Resting in his hotel room, he thought of Magdalena while looking up at the ceiling from his bed. He called her as promised, leaving a message on her voicemail asking when she would like to see his house. She rang Charlie after her school day finished and suggested straight away. He arrived on time and saw her waiting by the front door. He smelt her perfume as he leant closer to her to unlock the door. Thoughts of happy married domesticity entered his head. They both looked around the ground floor before going upstairs. Charlie knew the best features of the house were the balcony views. Walking through the main double bedroom, Magdalena remarked, "Ah good, big bedroom for making family." He smiled in response to her plain speaking and anxious to see her first reaction when reaching the balcony.

"Oh, how wonderful, you have the best view in Bulgaria. It's gorgeous and you are so lucky," she gushed when stepping out onto it. Charlie looked at her as she leant on the rail, like Vanya earlier in Bonkas. The impact of the view always silenced the viewer after making their initial remarks. Charlie allowed her to look in silence while deciding to step closer to her. He felt drawn without planning what to do as he inched closer to her. His mind was battling to find a suitable gesture of affection to test her reaction – hopefully a positive one too. He was a breath away from her when he decided to put a hand on her shoulder. Hopefully it would provoke that favourable response. It was a harmless gesture, and he knew it wouldn't create any panic reaction should she disapprove. He couldn't imagine her screaming, then seeing farmers running with pitchforks to her rescue. That, all over a harmless placing of his hand on her shoulder. However, just as he came to within an inch of hand touching shoulder, she suddenly moved.

Pointing while turning, she said, "My parents live just over there and that's where I grew up." Charlie quickly dropped his hand and suddenly remembered Mr 'Evro' was her father and he was just across the way.

"Ah no, that's killed it, I bet he's looking across at us now, probably through a pair of binoculars too," he thought. The moment was lost.

Charlie would have to wait until another time to test Magdalena's affection. He complimented her father and she surprised Charlie by confirming his innocence regarding the theft of the taxi. He'd temporarily forgotten she knew about it. Both laughed at that misunderstanding and continued chatting with high spirits, then went downstairs to leave. Just before they said their goodbyes, Charlie remembered something he was meaning to ask her since the restaurant night. "Oh, by the way, what's your father's name?" he asked.

"Valentino, or Valio to you because you know him now," she replied with a smile. They stood looking at each other for three whole seconds without a further word. It registered a mutual attraction and Charlie felt secure in having a second 'bite of the apple' and making a physical sign of affection. He moved his head forward to kiss her cheek. She responded favourably by offering it. His lips on her soft cheek, together with her sweet smell, took him as close to paradise as thought possible. He promised to call her again on his next visit. They parted to walk their separate ways, both simultaneously turning heads to look over their shoulders. Each gave a wave just before going out of sight of the other.

He prepared to leave for London the next afternoon and promised Petar and Rumyana he'd stay with them for his next visit. Thinking of the socks and the night in the restaurant with the women, he said, "I'm looking forward to wearing the socks this coming winter," Petar gave Charlie a smile while Charlie returned an enquiring one. He hoped his look at Petar signalled an uncertainty about the true intentions for that evening drink. Despite his doubt he said, "I'd consider marrying the ugliest woman in the region, but not just for socks. It would have to be for a wardrobe of knitwear." All laughed and said their goodbyes.

Up to now, his flights to and from Bulgaria were uneventful except for the first outbound and return. They were novelty ones, having been his first trip to the country. Observing the habits of some Bulgarian passengers provided a bit of fun. This flight also would not be forgotten, but for a different reason. After he sat down into his aisle seat, he settled into reading the flight magazine. His neighbouring seat was occupied by a peaceful, quiet woman. The food and drinks trolley arrived sometime into the flight and the woman next to Charlie bought a coffee. That was when a mild irritation surfaced in Charlie, though one he would later regret! Her hands shook while she struggled to open the sachet of sugar. Holding the coffee at the same time didn't help. Charlie watched her out of the corners of his eyes hoping she'd eventually master the manoeuvrer. He was keen to get back to his magazine article and was growing impatient with her struggle. The situation was looking more precarious, and he was convinced her coffee was about to land on his lap. Deciding to take charge, he put the magazine down, took her coffee and sugar to mix both without a word. He picked up his magazine to continue reading but a few seconds later thought, "Tch, what I did was rude, despite it being a help. I shouldn't have just taken the coffee out of her hand without even asking," Looking away from the magazine and towards her again, he asked her if the coffee was all right. He hoped it would dispel any negative opinion she might have had of his earlier abrupt taking charge of her situation.

"Yes, it's okay, thanks. Sorry for my fumbling, I have a brain tumour and it makes handling things tricky."

An immediate self-loathing came over him after hearing her explanation. "Oh no, I'm so sorry, I shouldn't have just taken your coffee like that, and it was very rude of me. I'm sorry," he said apologetically. She made light of it and said he did her a favour. They continued to speak for most of the flight about her condition and their similar interests in Bulgaria. He felt she sensed enough sincerity from him to gamble saying to her, "I'm Funble by name and you're fumble by nature." They gave a small laugh and Charlie felt redeemed and wished her the best as the plane landed.

Next day, Nelly was in the upstairs back room looking out at Ms Belcher dead-heading her roses. She was throwing the offcuts over the fence into the neighbour's garden. "Bitch, and she talks to them as though she is pure as a priest. Huh, pure as my 'priest' who came here maybe," she snarled. Looking at Sue's bad-mindedness lessened Nelly's guilt about arranging the fake exorcism. While continuing to watch in silence, she suddenly heard someone say, "Boo," behind her. Jumping from fright and turning around, she saw Charlie grinning. "Charlie you monster, you frightened the life out of me. Did you bring me back anything this time?" she said cheekily.

"Hello Nelly, I wanted to sneak up on Andy but saw you here and decided to scare you instead. How come you're in today?" he asked.

"I'm here nearly every day now. She has me doing everything. They both are so lazy and the only thing I haven't been asked do is wipe their arses. If I'm asked to do that, then that's when I leave. Oh, she makes up reasons to deduct money from my wages too, the *kopele*!" she replied.

"*Kopele*?" Charlie enquired. Then continuing, "Actually no need, I think I have a good idea what that means. Anyway, I did bring you a present and not one but two. A cow bell to hang around your neck and a smaller one for your wrist. The cow bell will let Ms Belcher know when you are walking and the small bell for when you are working," he joked.

The two laughed and she stuck her tongue out at him. "You can keep them. Actually no, put them on the bottles of wine, so they both know who's drinking the most. They're alcoholics, Charlie," she said, eager to continue. "Listen, I must tell you about what I found in a drawer one day,"

"Okay, fine, but I want to check up on the loft first. Oh, I meant to say, your hair looks different, it's nice," he replied.

He walked up the new stairs to the loft and said, "Hi," to Andy. He was on his own again because most of the work was completed and the loft was at painting stage. The two talked and joked a little. Charlie wanted to talk about

Bulgaria but decided to still keep any mention of it just for Nelly's ears. Both were by the dormer window looking down at Ms Belcher reading in the garden. Nelly was pegging the last sheet of bed linen on the clothesline. They turned away from the window to face and admire the new work. Charlie stroked the new plaster walls and switched the downlighters on and off to admire. Then suddenly, a scream was heard from the garden. Both rushed to the window and saw Ms Belcher lying on the grass after falling off her sun lounger.

Nelly rushed over to help while Ms Belcher was shouting, "Go away, you bitch, you're still after me, haunting me, torturing me. Fuck off, I tell you, leave me alone, stay in Derbyshire. We need the priest again, get the priest for the loft," she screamed.

Charlie and Andy heard what was said as they had already flung open one of the dormer windows. They were surprised to see Nelly still standing over her and apparently not affected by her aggressive verbal attack. A neighbour was heard saying, "Awful woman, disgusting way to treat a hard-working home help."

Charlie left the loft and looked over the upstairs balcony to wait for Nelly or Dick to explain the chaotic scene. He saw Nelly climb the stairs with a mischievous smile on her face. "What have you done now, Nelly?" he asked.

"Oh it was nothing. She's mad and I didn't think she'd react that way," she replied.

"What do you mean? Explain!" he demanded. Just as she was about to speak, Dick came up the stairs with a bloodied towel and neck with a half-shaven beard.

"I was having a shave in the shed and nearly cut my bloody throat when Sue screamed. It was another one of her attacks," he exclaimed. On entering his study, he was heard saying, "Stupid bitch," as he closed the door. The two moved further away from the study door to speak.

"You know, that's a good name for a band and I must tell Tagaby," said Charlie with a change of mood.

"What?" she asked while frowning.

"'A shave in the shed', it has a ring to it, good name for a band," he replied.

"Yes, funny, ha-ha', she said mockingly. Then continuing, she said, "Anyway, let me explain, a week ago I was cleaning her desk and noticed a key in the lock of a drawer. That drawer was always locked without a key in it. So, she must have forgotten it that time and I decided to have a look. I found two pictures of herself when young. In one she was naked and leaning on a cow with backside sticking out to whoever took the picture. The other one showed her wearing lose clothing and lying in hay in a sexy way. You get me? Oh, and her hair was like mine now. On the back of one picture was written 'To my Ponytail, from your Stallion'. What does 'ponytail' mean?"

"Phew, seriously, a picture of her naked? The ponytail comment must be referring to her hairdo. I wonder who the stallion lover was? Can't be Dick, as he's a duck."

The two laughed and Nelly continued explaining. "Anyway, this is the best bit. I now know about her loopy mad attacks and past youth haunting her. So, I dressed up in the same clothes as her in that second picture and arranged my hair the same way too. That's why you noticed me different."

"Okay, but what has it got to do with her outburst just now?" asked Charlie.

"I thought it might start one of her fits if I dressed up like her in that picture and walk around the garden. Also, I never told you, she started drinking the bottle of Rakia you brought me. She was drinking it at time of her fit, she's often a bit drunk," said Nelly.

"Yes, maybe the combination of booze and your likeness to her demon sent her into a fit. Nelly, you're wicked. So, she really thought you were her devil past coming to torment her. Phew, she's really gone in the head now," he said. The two stood in silence for a few seconds to dwell on the strange and disturbing episode in the garden. Then Charlie said, "Mm, I wonder can she write with her mouth?"

"What?" Nelly replied quizzically.

"Well, if she ends up in a straitjacket before this loft is finished, she won't be able to sign a cheque to pay me."

Despite not knowing what a straitjacket was, Nelly sensed Charlie was ridiculing Ms Belcher. It made Nelly feel as though she was excused from her earlier misdemeanour, resulting in her to smile and retort, "Ha, look who's wicked now, Charlie."

Chapter 8

While sitting at home that evening, Charlie felt an impending doom regarding his house in Bulgaria. Earlier in the afternoon, he had read about tremors recently recorded in the southwest of the country. His house was in the middle of that region. Sitting staring at the television but not registering what was showing, he imagined his house collapsing! He focused more and more on it while staring at the screen. People and places from his five trips came into mind in a disorderly sequence like a flashback. He paused on each face he saw in his mind's eye and coupled each one with earthquakes. He dreamt he was discussing the house with Borka while both standing in front of it. He asked how earthquake proof it was. Borka replied with a huge laugh to ridicule the question, while at the same time a loud rumble came from the ground. Borka still laughed despite both nearly falling over from being shaken by a tremor. He stubbornly ignored it and asked Charlie to speak up because he cannot hear him.

Next to pop into Charlie's mind was Magdalena. He imagined the earthquake was her fault because of her voracious and wild lovemaking. The municipality formed a task committee called 'Action Magdalena'. Its purpose being to find a solution for a non-reoccurrence of the quakes. The committee asked her to take sedatives to control her arousals. Or, would she move to a less Geo active part of the country for lovemaking. Finally, he imagined Mr 'Evro' (Valio) telling his wife to stop singing in case she was causing the tremors.

He was distracted from his dreaming by hearing a similar sounding word to Magdalena coming from the television. Quickly refocusing on the screen, he saw a news article on a church named St Mary of Magdalene. It held no further interest, and he switched thoughts back to his house again. Though the impact of his recent thoughts of impending doom lessened to one of only a growing concern, nevertheless, it was still enough of a concern for him to decide to book another flight. Besides, he felt a growing need to check if faults were corrected, or at least started. Also, the water and electric connection works needed new paperwork permissions and he wanted to know if Borka was preparing them. He could fly any time because the loft job was free of problems, so he booked to go for the following week. He switched off the television and went to bed. While waiting to go to sleep, he wondered if his pessimism was justified. He was convinced that having a permanent state of pessimism was healthy. He believed it prepared a person to accept and therefore deal with any unforeseen challenges throughout life. A kind of good default trait. Then he recalled how someone had said, "A mere mortal could not anticipate fate." It comforted Charlie to think that if he thought the worst, then it wouldn't happen. Though thinking again, but in a less superstitious manner, he thought, "No, don't be silly, there will be no earthquake. Maybe at most a floor quake under Magdalena's bed." He drifted off to sleep.

Again, landing in Sofia, he wasted no time travelling down to Ovineshta. He checked into Hotel Rumyana as promised and decided to go straight to his house. As he walked out of the hotel, Rumyana called him and said, "Hello Charlie, we are going to be neighbours."

"Sorry?" asked Charlie.

"We are building a hotel on the plot opposite your house, on the other corner," she explained.

"Ah, I see, that's great. We'll both have someone from whom to borrow sugar, should we ever run out," he joked.

It was her turn to say, "Sorry" from her confusion.

"Oh, never mind, it's an English saying," he replied. He made his excuse to leave and walked the stony riverbank towards his house. As it came into view, he became sullen at the thought of a hotel appearing near his house. He cherished his unobstructed view of the mountains even more so now, knowing one day it would become partly obscured. That was despite him being sure Petar and Rumyana would be nice neighbours. Purposely slowing his walk as he approached the house, he wondered if anyone was working inside. He didn't hear any noise on arriving at the front door and anticipated the worst. It was locked, meaning no workers were inside. He unlocked it, entered and scanned the same view as on his previous visit. No further work had been done since his last trip. As he locked the door to leave, he decided to go to Bonkas and plan his next action regarding Borka and the remaining work. Aimlessly strolling around the streets, he came upon an estate agent and immediately thought of his house's value. Going in to leave details for a valuation distracted him from the lingering irritation of an abandoned site. Despite the house not being finished, a valuation could be given from what had been done.

  He arrived back in Ovineshta just after lunchtime and decided to call Borka. Scanning for a comfortable spot, he chose a quiet *mehana* on the edge of the square. A comfortable seat was important for he envisaged himself sitting for a long time. The routine for contacting Borka involved making several calls before a possibility of one being answered. He sat back and stretched his legs before dialling and patiently waited for a reply. Staring across the square and listening to countless ringing tones was how the following hour played out. Borka was not answering. Thankfully the monotony of that hour was broken by a strange occurrence on the other side of the square. He was staring at the corner from where he walked to his plot and saw a Bonkas taxi stop. A woman passenger got out, went into a hardware shop and returned to the taxi with two large tins of paint. The taxi drove off up one of the fork roads. A while later it returned to the square with the same woman passenger, and exited the other side. The behaviour looked normal, and it provided Charlie with a distraction from his endless telephoning. Ten minutes after the taxi left, he saw a man appear at the same corner and go into the hardware shop. Raised voices were heard coming from it and Charlie wondered if it was an argument. It was and the man came out, followed by a woman to continue their furious exchanges. Their voices echoed around the square, then suddenly stopped when he gave her a dismissive wave and walked away. The woman returned to her shop. Charlie wondered if the woman in the taxi and the two arguing were in some way connected.

Walking back to his hotel he pondered over what he had just seen. Rumyana was in the hall when he arrived, and he recounted to her what he'd just seen. She knew all three characters and the background story causing the argument. "Yes, all three are connected and it's terrible what happened to create the hatred. I'll tell you the story," she said.

Charlie became more intrigued and his eagerness to understand the mystery was a welcome distraction from Borka.

She continued, "Before I start, excuse any bad English and best I explain in simple terms. The woman you saw buying paint and the man are married. He came here from Plovdiv few months ago to build a hotel and to manage it with family. The family decided to start new life in the countryside – you understand?" she asked.

"Yes perfectly, carry on," he replied.

"Okay, he rented a room in town for one year to supervise building and paid all the rent at beginning. The landlady was shocked by his arrangement but happy for all the money. His wife and family stayed in Plovdiv. Six weeks after husband moved in with landlady, his wife decided to pay a secret, sorry, I mean, surprise visit. She called at the house where he stayed, but he or landlady was not in. She then went to the building site thinking he might be working late, but not there. Then the problem started," she said.

"Oh yes, what you mean?" he eagerly enquired.

"She decided to go for a meal that evening before going back to hotel. She saw her husband and landlady eating at a table in same restaurant," she said.

"Oh no," replied Charlie.

"Oh yes, she didn't say anything but just looked or spied on them. Husband and landlady were eating, drinking, laughing and you know, having good time," she said.

"Hang on, Rumyana, how did you find out about all this?" asked Charlie. "I know the hardware shop keeper and she tell me," she replied.

"Ah, okay. Hang on though, how did the shop keeper find out? Ah don't tell me, the husband told her?" he asked.

"No, it was the postman," she replied.

"Mm, okay, but hang on again, who told… oh forget it, carry on," he said.

"Okay, the wife come here again in evening to spy on husband and see if he and landlady go out again. They did and she found them in another restaurant doing more jokey, laughing, drinking, eating. Wife decided husband having affair, goes back home to plan revenge," she said. Rumyana paused for a moment to draw breath.

Charlie used the break to say, "Yes, definitely an affair because they started laughing before any eating or drinking on the second date. Always a bad sign." Rumyana hadn't understood Charlie's attempt at humour and carried on with the story.

"Okay, her revenge is with paint. One day she came to hardware shop by taxi, buys paint to throw over new hotel work, then taxi drives her away. This been going on up to now," she said.

"Okay, fine, but what about the husband and the hotel? He must be going mad at the disruption? Also, is he really having an affair?" asks Charlie.

"Yes, he's very upset and says he is not having an affair. He says that the landlady gave him good discount on rent because he paid a year's rent in one payment – understand? He takes her for meals to show thanks. Wife doesn't believe him. One day she went to hotel site and screamed, 'You are getting fat, you bastard, because too much eating, jokey, laughing with whore. You should be losing weight, you bastard, from stress and work on hotel.' Then she spits. She has good English, you see?" she said.

"Phew, that's a terrible misunderstanding between two people," replied Charlie.

"Yes, but there is always a winner in everything, Charlie," she stressed.

"Oh, who's that then?" he enquired.

"The hardware shop, of course. She is making much money selling paint to his wife. Clever businesswoman, too. She offers a discount with every two tins she buys.

Everyone in town is laughing and saying the hotel will be painted before it is built," she said and the two immediately allowing themselves a guilty laugh. She continued, "Even cleverer because store woman told the husband she can stock chemical paint remover and give him a discount for every two tins he buys. So, Charlie, you see how even small wars make money for some people. The longer the war, the more money hardware shop woman makes.

"Finally Charlie, about the postman, he spreads lies to keep the war going. Every time wife hears lies, she buys paint to throw and husband buys chemical remover to clean," she said.

"Mm, it's not nice really and it ruins lives, as well as new walls. Ha!" he said while expecting a laugh from Rumyana. She didn't. He continued, "Why don't you stop it by telling the wife the truth about all the lying?"

"No, no, Charlie, I get a discount too from hardware shop. I tell her I only threatening to tell truth and ruin her money-making from paint."

"You're as bad as them," he exclaimed.

"Don't worry, everything has turned out okay. Let me explain. I hear husband now started affair with landlady because crazy wife behaviour and now very happy. Wife started affair with taxi driver because of many taxi rides and he feel sorry for her, comfort her – you see? He owns the taxi company, nice man and has money. So, all are happy," she said with a smile.

"Incredible, just incredible!" replied Charlie. After further thought, he added, "I imagine the postman and hardware shop owner pray every night he doesn't get a bicycle puncture the next day."

"Oh why?" she asked with a quizzical look.

"So that he won't be delayed pedalling his money-making gossip for the day," he said while knowing she wouldn't understand the pun. Nevertheless, he smiled and quickly added, "Get it?" referring to the pun.

The only reply he received was, "Are you okay, Charlie?"

"Never mind," he replied.

They both simultaneously drew in air and sighed, relieved to know all was successfully explained by her and understood by him. Conveniently at that moment, his phone rang. "Ah, I bet that's Borka," he exclaimed. It wasn't.

"Hello Mr Funble, this is Nadia of Bonkas Sales and Rentals, hope you are well. I'm calling you because I have an enquiry about your house," she said.

"Ah hello, Nadia, that was quick. I'm surprised to hear of interest so quickly," Charlie replied.

"He is someone who knows and likes your town. He is always looking for an investment there. Will it be okay to give him your contact details?" she requested.

"Yes, that's fine, Nadia, thank you," he replied.

Rumyana watched and listened to the conversation, then asked with surprise, "So you are going to sell your house? How can you? You have no curtains." she exclaimed.

Charlie smiled at her endearing comment about the lack of curtains and replied, "Ha, yes, you're right and no, I'm not going to sell. I was fed up this morning about my builder's disappearance. He hasn't worked on the house for quite a while. So, I went for a valuation of the house to cheer me up and for curiosity, too, that's all," he replied.

"What about curtains? I know a very good curtain maker, she is expert," she said.

"Okay, great and thank you, I can at least get the upstairs windows done. What's her number?" he enquired. After taking her number, he went up to his room to rest and mull over the day's events.

His heart suddenly skipped a beat as thoughts of Magdalena entered his head while lying on his bed. He was surprised he hadn't thought of her all day. He pushed her image to the margins of his mind, for Charlie had a more serious issue to solve. One of getting Borka to return to working on his house.

While thinking of a resolution to his problem, his phone rang again. "Surely that must be Borka this time," he said. It wasn't. It was a Mr Kreatin calling about his house for sale advert. Arrangements were made for the two to meet in Bonkas the next day. Charlie was eager to discuss his house after hearing Mr Kreatin tell him he worked for the government. That single fact alone seemed like hope for Charlie. He planned to use the house sale as a ruse for his ulterior motive of coaxing Mr Kreatin to help him. He hoped he'd oblige Charlie with any influence and power to bring Borka back to the house. He knew he could be overreacting to the inactivity with his house build. After all, he didn't know for what reason workers were absent. Despite that, he preferred to focus on a worst-case scenario and take as effective measures as possible to resume the flow of work. If there was a valid reason for a stop in construction, then he'd be happy to apologise.

The two met next morning outside a cafe and Mr Kreatin stood to greet Charlie as he approached his table. Charlie spoke first as they shook hands saying, "Hello Mr Kreatin, I'm Charlie Funble and nice to meet you."

Mr Kreatin smiled showing an expensive set of teeth and said, "The pleasure is mine, Mr Funble." Continuing with well-spoken English, he requested Charlie to pronounce his name correctly. "Please pronounce my name correctly, Charlie. When you speak it, it sounds like you're saying 'Kretin." Obviously, I do not want to be called a kretin."

"I understand, sorry," replied Charlie.

"I was in once in London for a meeting and everyone in the room kept addressing me as kretin instead of my proper name Kreatin. Very annoying," he stated.

Charlie would have burst out laughing, but for fear of an angry response from the huge man. He hid any indication of the probable truth that all in the room might have intended calling him kretin. He assumed he said or did something stupid for him to be thought of as one. A notable characteristic about his speech was his habit of rolling his 'r's' when saying 'Charlie'. Charlie was amazed at his tongue's dexterity. It was like the taxi driver on his first trip to Sofia airport. He remembered how he was able to stick his tongue out far while saying the word 'baby'. As they sat down, Charlie made a mental note to later practice saying Charlie while trying to roll the 'r' with his tongue. He had lived with the name 'Charlie' all his life and knew it was physically impossible for western tongues to achieve.

"So, Charlie, your house is of interest to me, how much are you asking for it?" he asked.

Charlie hesitated replying, because of suddenly realising he forgot to ask Nadia the price she'd chosen. A deceptive reply was needed and Charlie said, "Well, I think it best you see it first without any distraction from a price. Then we can talk about the money."

"Fine, we'll go now, if it's all right with you, Charlie," he suggested. It was ideal timing, as having Mr Kreatin stand inside the house was exactly where he wanted him. Charlie felt akin to a shepherd steering a sheep into a pen. When inside the house, he would ask him if he could help in getting Borka back on the job. While both approached the house in silence, Charlie reflected over the meeting so far and confirmed his earlier opinion of Mr Kreatin being an egoist. If right, he might agree to a request for help because it would massage that ego.

The two stepped into the house and Mr Kreatin was highly impressed with the views and style. Then he asked about the unfinished work and Charlie explained how

Borka had disappeared. Mr Kreatin responded with a reply which saved Charlie having to make the request for help. "He must come back and finish. He must, Charlie. I can and will help you," he exclaimed.

"Ah, that's fantastic of you to offer help, Mr Kreatin. Thanks ever so much," he replied while making extra effort in pronouncing his name correctly. "Can you meet me at the same table tomorrow morning to make a list of unfinished works?" he asked.

"Yes, for sure," he replied.

The two parted and Charlie headed back to his hotel. Being a man with a certain amount of pessimism, Charlie thought the meeting went too much in Mr Kreatin's favour. "I bet he'll want to get paid for his help. Mm, he probably shouldn't ask for money, too, seeing as he's a government civil servant. Surely it would count as a conflict of interest," he thought. He didn't dwell any longer on any possible financial commitments regarding the offer of help. It would diminish his joy of having someone notable offer their services to resume the build.

As he closed the door of his room, Magdalena's image came to mind again. He stood for a second to focus on her, but quickly dismissed it a second time. Another woman needed his attention, and it was the curtain lady – Evelina. It looked like no progress with building work would happen during this visit. So, organising the curtains would at least give some feeling of progress with the house. Evelina was fitting curtains in a Bonkas hotel the same time. He phoned her and a meeting was arranged for the next afternoon. Charlie went to bed with Mr Kreatin and Evelina on his mind. Though Magdalena too, for the third time and a regret of not calling her started to weigh on his mind. He consoled himself by thinking the delay might make her more eager to see him rather than forget him. The police poster then came to mind and the adage, 'Out of Sight Out of Mind'. He thought, "That's it, she has a picture of me and that'll keep me fresh in her mind. Mm, mind you, a picture on a police 'wanted' poster isn't the most endearing image of someone. Anyway, now she knows the poster was a huge mistake, it's no longer an issue."

As he walked towards the cafe next morning, Charlie saw Mr Kreatin's big, shiny bald head in the distance. He was reading paperwork which allowed Charlie to study him unnoticed. He looked tall even while sitting and gave the impression of a man living a charmed life. Hands were manicured and expensive-looking clothes hung off his huge body. On nearing him, Charlie saw he sat at two bistro tables he had pulled together and refusing a request from a couple to sit at one. The cafe was full of occupied tables, so the couple had to leave. Then a waiter came over to remonstrate with him. Mr Kreatin abruptly dismissed him with a wave of his big hand on the end of a long arm. His behaviour was unpleasant, and it signalled to Charlie a boorish, selfish manner. He thought it might be something to be wary of now that he would be in his company for an unknown period.

On arriving at his two tables, he stood up and greeted Charlie with a wide smile. Charlie looked at him with diminished respect and imagined a crocodile smiling back at him. "Good morning, Charlie, hope you had a wonderful night's sleep. Let me buy you a coffee," he said. His contrasting behaviour in that short period of time agitated Charlie. He felt he couldn't trust his amicable manner towards him being genuine and hoped his convivial attitude wasn't used to softened him up for a big bill!

"Good morning, Mr Kreatin," Charlie replied with perfect pronunciation of his name again. He was aware not to agitate Mr Kreatin to influence an unfavourable bill for services. After ordering two coffees, Mr Kreatin proceeded to write a list of all the remaining works while Charlie dictated them.

His anticipation of a bill was confirmed by Mr Kreatin saying, "Charlie, I can have this man back on your property and complete the works no problem. Also, I can obtain your water and electric connection permissions immediately. I hope you understand this is work and time, so a small fee is required," he stated with a part smile and part grin.

Charlie looked at his smiling face and thought the only difference between Mr Kreatin and a crocodile was the sweet smell of cologne from him. "Thank you and I understand about the fee. What figure do you have in mind?" Charlie replied.

"Oh, don't worry, I think we can keep it reasonable and say €12,000," he replied.

Charlie didn't agree or disagree but just concentrated on hiding his shock and said, "Mm, it's a lot of money."

"Well, I can make it €10,000 if it would help," he replied. Charlie agreed, thinking €10,000 was what he really wanted, and the two thousand extra was clever subterfuge.

Mr Kreatin helped softened the initial impact of the high bill for Charlie by reasoning he might be worse off if he didn't employ him. Obtaining the electricity and water connection agreements speedily would be a bonus and very much slower with Borka. Also, he guaranteeing Borka's return to the house seemed like an act of magic now. While equating his help in euros was impossible, he felt €10,000 was extortionate, as well as illegal. So, Mr Kreatin was the bigger winner in the deal. Charlie's earlier observation of him writing the list confirmed his inappropriate behaviour. He shook his hand – noticeably – while writing, to change the appearance of his handwriting style. Charlie was sure it was to safeguard himself from any possible future accusation. He could deny writing it should any authority question improper use of his position. They arranged another meet-up the next day to apply for and collect the water and electric connection permissions. The two parted and Charlie walked around town until his appointment with Evelina.

While sitting outside the chosen cafe before meeting her, he thought about organza. He saw a lot of the material used for hotel curtains during his earlier walk around town. It gave him something to think about while waiting for her, as he was sure she'd suggest the material. In a short while, a woman stopped outside the cafe looking for someone. Charlie looked at her and called her over. "Hello, are you Evelina?" he asked.

"Yes, and I guess you are Charlie?" she replied.

"Yes, we've found each other," he said. He was happy to be in the company of a woman. It made a change from the overbearing Mr Kreatin. Charlie hoped she wasn't in a hurry as they ordered drinks. "This is my second meeting today. My previous one was about recalling my builder to finish my house. Someone has offered to return him, but for a fee," he said.

Her eyes widened and mouth opened in surprise and said, "Oh be very careful when employing services of strangers here in Bulgaria. You are a foreigner and many gangsters here would love to take your money. You said 'return'. It makes the builder sound like a package. Nothing horrible will be done to him, I hope. He won't be delivered in a coffin?" she enquired with a wry smile.

He liked her sense of humour and for understanding the peculiarities of the English language. "Oh, my word no, no and sorry – I used the wrong words. I meant he'll be encouraged to come back and finish building my house," he hastily replied. The opening conversation was friendly and continued to flow to a level normally found much later between initial strangers. "You must be well established seeing as you are working on hotels here in Bonkas," he asked.

"I have work to keep me going but it's not the real me. I'm a painter, a fine art painter," she explained.

"Ah sounds wonderful, but why make curtains?" he asked.

"Being a fine artist doesn't always provide a steady income for the whole year. I tried my best to make life work, but it didn't, so now I make curtains," she replied.

"Such a pity, seeing as you have a great talent," Charlie's genuine regret for her misfortune in work direction, prompted her to embellish on her painting.

"Charlie, can I tell you something? I'm married to an alcoholic and it was a big problem. He would drink all night and not work our little farm during the day. So, I suggested I make him my model for portrait scenes and paint him at night. It kept him out of the bars for a couple weeks. He was sober and the farm work was done. Then he started drinking during the days and the farm work suffered again. Not wanting to give up, I suggested he work the farm and start his drinking straight after he finished, but at home in the kitchen. He agreed and would fall asleep on the kitchen table by late evening. While asleep, I created scenes with his body, like putting a dead rabbit on his lap and a shotgun by his side to mimic a wounded poacher. I just added the necessary colour of blood to my picture. I'd create other scenes too and it intrigued him to know in which theme my painting depicted him. I never revealed the painting until I finished it, and he enjoyed the anticipation of the final work," she explained.

"This is surreal and great. So, what happened then?" Charlie eagerly asked.

"Things got worse again. He became fed up with drinking at home and wanted to return to the bars. I knew I couldn't cope with the strain and feared our marriage would end. With that in mind I did one last painting of him for my insurance," she said.

"What do you mean by insurance?" asked Charlie.

"I'm in Sofia now and have a young child. If we were to separate, I need to know he would help with money. So, when my husband fell asleep for my last painting, I put lipstick and eyeliner on him and a baby's dummy in his mouth. Also, I put one of my bras tucked inside his open shirt to look like he was wearing it. Oh, I shaped his hand to hold my daughter's doll too. Then I took a picture of him and afterwards returned him back to normal. I can threaten to show the picture to his friends or family if he doesn't help me with our child. You see, men are generally very masculine here in Bulgaria. Such pictures would create a scandal – especially in small rural areas. Besides, if he doesn't care about his friends seeing the picture, I can tell him I'll show it to the authorities and say he's a cross dresser and unstable or nutty. He won't want to be locked up," she explained enthusiastically.

Her story sent a chill down Charlie's back, despite the hot day. He stared at her and nodded slowly, to convey serious attention to her story. The truth was he was unable to think of any reply from being so shocked from hearing her deviousness. He never previously had to responded to anything so outrageously contrived. Realising he couldn't go on nodding; he thought a change of subject was the best way forward. Wearing a slightly stunned look he said, "Would you like another coffee, Evelina?" It wasn't an interesting change in conversation but at least it took their focus off a drunk husband and her conniving. Evelina appeared more confident after telling her story and Charlie saw her newly found resolve. He sensed her manifestation of a personal and embarrassing experience gave her relief and an empowerment to carry on with life.

"No thank you, let's go to your house to measure up for the curtains," she replied. Charlie was glad to stand up and to be freed from the constraints of the table and her scary tale.

Approaching his house, she gushed, "What a beautiful house, Charlie."

"Yes, I'm proud of it, but of course it's not finished," he replied. The house had over thirty small windows, which was more than usually seen in a house of its size. He wondered was her excitement truly because of registering potential earnings from the sight of so many windows. They measured all of them and she said she'd phone the next day with a quote. She used a clever ploy to save money by buying her materials in Istanbul once every few months. After their parting, Charlie walked back to his room and finally called Magdalena. Sitting down comfortably on his bed, he dialled with no reply.

Ten minutes later he received a text saying, "*Hello Charlie, how are you? I'm in Sofia visiting my sister*."

Reading it, he thought, "Mm, I should have got in touch sooner." Charlie wouldn't be seeing her on this trip and lay down to think of the next day with Mr Kreatin, before going to sleep.

Chapter 9

They greeted each other on meeting at the same cafe, with a wary waiter looking at Mr Kreatin. "Good morning, Charlie, I hope you had a pleasant night's sleep," said Mr Kreatin.

Charlie wanted to test his real temperament by saying something unpredictable. Polite protocol always created a harmonious unproblematic discourse between people. However, it didn't allow either to know the other's true tolerance. "Actually, I didn't because the thought of your bill kept me awake," Charlie replied.

They looked at each other for two seconds before Mr Kreatin burst out laughing. Charlie laughed too, but only to disguise his distaste for him. The laugh was more of a wince, like one seen on someone's face after smelling something horrible! Charlie was glad that Mr Kreatin had a sense of humour. Though, he did wonder if it was really a mock sense of humour, used to mitigate any unpleasant interactions with anyone not liking him. He didn't want to test his theory in case of provoking a nasty response should he be wrong. "So, Charlie, about the fee, can you pay me now before we commence with obtaining the permissions?" he asked with a smile.

"Ah well, I thought I'd transfer the money when back in London. I can't get that amount of cash now," he replied.

"What do you have in cash?"

"I can give you a thousand leva," he replied meekly.

He took the money from Charlie. Then, sticking his tongue out as quick as a lizard, licked a thumb to count the money. Satisfied, he said, "Okay, Charlie, I'll get the permissions, but you know they can be cancelled until I receive the remaining money. I hope you understand?" It was followed by an awkward laugh, more fake than genuine, he then said unconvincingly, "I'm only joking." Charlie understood the warning and from that moment onwards, his disdain for him deepened. He wished he had the courage to address him as Kretin from here on.

"Okay, let's go to the electric company first," said Mr Kreatin. It was a short walk away and as they approached the entrance, Mr Kreatin put on a pair of sunglasses. They made him look menacing. Charlie knew they were a prop to help him receive a quick compliance to his requests from staff. They arrived at a desk and Mr Kreatin showed staff his government I.D. card while standing like a bouncer. Then he spoke a few assertive words, reducing a staff member to looking like a misbehaving pupil summoned to a headmaster. She obediently pulled Charlie's file from the bottom of a towering pile and proceeded to fill it in.

Walking out of the electric company, Mr Kreatin said, "Now we go for the water."

Charlie was in awe of what he had just seen and how power, position or connections could make life a lot easier. He thought, "In my case, it was literally a case of connections get connections."

The same routine played out with the water permissions. After leaving the building, Mr Kreatin took off his sunglasses and flashed a winner's smile to Charlie. Charlie couldn't help raising a smile in return – albeit a small one – in appreciation.

"Now, the builder. I can have him in Ovineshta for a meeting tomorrow by using some encouragement. Like for instance, an investigation into his tax or whatever. What is his number?"

Charlie gave him his number while suddenly regretting how things were taking this course. He now hoped that Borka had abandoned the work for good because of the severe retribution Mr Kreatin had planned. He also reminded himself of all the remaining work to be done on the house. Both those things helped justify his course of action. It was a lot – the structural post with the split must be changed. There was all the manual work in supplying the property with water and electric. Then finally, the time-consuming work to obtain the title deeds, so he could call himself rightful owner. Borka had a lot to do, and it was the wrong time for him to be disappearing. He knew he had other building projects ongoing which he might be prioritising. It further convinced Charlie he couldn't take a gamble and just wait for him to turn up again.

Mr Kreatin finished his call and said, "Tomorrow at one pm in Ovineshta at your hotel and you'll need a translator for my conversation with Borka."

"Okay, I understand and thank you. I'll get one for tomorrow," Charlie replied.

They parted and Charlie's mind became a whirlwind of thoughts about the next day's meeting. "Will Borka turn up? If he does, will he be late and drunk again? Will he become vexed from being told what to do, resulting in a fight? Will I be a source of gossip and ignored by the town's people in the future? I already got off to a bad start over that stolen taxi misunderstanding," he thought worryingly. He walked aimlessly around Bonkas for the rest of the day to worry about the meeting. Again, he thought if he worried enough, nothing untoward would happen and all would go smoothly to end satisfactorily. A while into his rambling around Bonkas, a most unexpected and helpful chance meeting occurred. He came across the teacher he met at the end of that scary car journey with Petar and friends in Ovineshta. He asked her to translate for him the next day and she agreed.

On finally deciding to return to his room, his phone rang and it was Evelina. "Hello Charlie, it's Evelina. How did things go this morning?" she asked.

"Hello Evelina, fine, thanks, I have both water and electric connection permissions now. Also, a meeting with the builder is arranged for tomorrow," he replied.

"Oh, that's good news. I thought I'd call you before I send the quote. If you're happy with it, I can make the curtains here in Sofia. Then visit your house one day to fit them. You're welcome to stop by my place here in Sofia whenever you're passing," she said.

"Thanks, and I'll keep that in mind. Yes, I'll text you straight back about the quote," he said. He was in no mood to speak with anyone on a social level until the meeting was over. Evelina's open invite to see her in Sofia faded from his mind as quick as he heard it.

Finally arriving back in his room in Ovineshta, he stared at the mirror for no particular reason. He stood thinking about the meeting with tempers possibly raised, he imagined Borka and Kreatin fighting. With this in mind, he did some stretching and spontaneously threw two lazy punches into the space in front. Standing still again and looking in the mirror, he muttered, "You idiot, don't be silly. What am I doing? I'll just stick close to Kreatin and he can take a few punches for me if Borka loses his cool. He's being paid enough for his trouble. I can buy any plasters for any cuts he might receive." A fly entered the room and would have been easy to squash. Though for fear of tempting fate for the next day's showdown, he resisted the temptation to kill it. He rather chose the annoying job of chasing it back out of the window. The darkness fell and knowing he'd have a restless night, he went to bed late.

Looking at the bright, sunny morning on waking, Charlie was at ease, though anxiety would eventually return about the impending showdown. He had breakfast and lounged around the hotel, finally resting in the foyer at noon. At twelve-thirty pm Mr Kreatin arrived. While looking for Charlie, he dropped his car keys and was noticeably slow while bending to pick them up. Finally standing upright again, he picked and tugged his upper clothing to make himself comfortable again. It piqued Charlie's curiosity as he never gave the impression of being stiff or not supple. Also, his adjustment of clothing seemed to take an unnaturally long time. Being in an apprehensive mood about the meeting, he was convinced Mr Kreatin was wearing a bulletproof vest.

Panic and turmoil rolled inside Charlie's head and he thought, "Oh my god, that's it, he's wearing a bulletproof vest under his shirt. There's going to be a shoot-out over this snagging list, I just know it. It's a hot day with hot heads, I bet guns will be drawn when the split post is mentioned. Changing that is a big job and Borka won't want to do it. I bet a drunk Borka turns up and Kreatin becomes angry. Then, along with the hot day all hell will break lose."

Eventually seeing Charlie, Mr Kreatin called, "Hello Charlie, we best go upstairs to the balcony area as there's more room for the meeting."

Charlie obediently followed him upstairs and thought, "Of course he wants to go up here. It's so any blood spilt won't ruin the foyer's wooden floor. The balcony is tiled and easier for mopping up blood spills. Maybe Petar and Rumyana told him so. Oh no, what have I let myself in for?" Shortly after sitting, the teacher – Emily – arrived.

Rumyana came onto the balcony with her and asked everyone what they wanted for drinks. "A pint of Dutch courage," Charlie said with a nervous laugh. No one understood him and drinks were ordered.

The waiting started for the accused and it continued with many sighs, groans and tuts from Mr Kreatin. He was sitting at the table end by the edge of the balcony, with arms resting on top alongside an A4 pad of notes and pen. The seat opposite was left for Borka while Emily and Charlie sat at the other end. All three waited... and waited... and waited in silence. The sound of an axe splitting wood by a man below the balcony was the only noise to puncture the silence.

"He might be useful up here later if things get tense or violent," said Charlie making another nervous attempt at humour. Emily smiled but Mr Kreatin remained sullen faced and annoyed at having to wait. Eventually all decided Borka wouldn't show up. The tense mood eased into a more relaxed chatty one because of their decision. That was despite knowing the meeting was only postponed and would happen sometime. Then, just as Rumyana appeared and asked about more drinks, a car's tyres were heard tearing into the gravel on the roadside below. It parked at a rebellious angle giving the impression its driver was arrogant, agitated or at least careless. Everyone on the balcony craned their heads to look through and over the balustrade to see who it was. Borka had arrived.

Two minutes later a stern-faced Borka stepped onto the balcony and stood in silence to look at Mr Kreatin. He gave a slight nod and walked past Charlie and Emily to sit down opposite him. Both men sat with straightened backs like bull walruses preparing to charge each other.

Mr Kreatin sucked in a breath to announce himself. With an equally stern face he said in Bulgarian, "Hello Borka, we spoke on the phone already. You can call me Mr Kreatin."

Next, the most unpredictable response came from Borka. He laughed and slumped back into his seat and said, "Ha, I know someone, same name and he called Kretin."

Emily translated for Charlie who immediately felt the tension release its grip on him. Borka's laugh had instantly defused the situation. He hoped Mr Kreatin wouldn't challenge Borka over the ridiculing of his name, which had eased initial hostilities. He didn't and the only threatening behaviour was a return to their stern faces.

Borka ordered a drink and conversation commenced between Mr Kreatin and himself, with Charlie and Emily looking on. Demands were made by Mr Kreatin, to which he received angry responses from Borka. At one point, he threw half his drink over the balcony in a fit of rage. It was followed by a shout from below. More drinks were ordered and more of the snag list discussed. Again, an angry Borka threw half of his next drink over the balcony, followed by another shout from below. Emily whispered the translation while Charlie only partially heard. No matter, because he knew from the length of discussions that all snags must've been covered. He remained especially attentive for a mention of the split post, as that was a priority and urgently needed replacing. Emily confirmed it being mentioned but said Borka only mumbled an inaudible reply. Borka threw his last drink over the balcony – followed by another shout from below. Then, everyone stood up to leave.

While walking down the stairs, Charlie asked Emily if she knew Magdalena, seeing as she was also a teacher in town.

"Yes, I know her and I must tell you she has spoken about you. She's still in Sofia with her sister," she said.

He was happy to hear she was with her sister and not a boyfriend. "Oh right, thanks, Emily, I'll give her a call," he replied.

As the four walked out of the hotel, Charlie looked at the man chopping wood at the entrance. He stopped working to give a long nasty look at Borka and Mr Kreatin as they passed by. Charlie noticed the back of the man's shirt was soaked and it was too wet to be sweat. Walking past, he smelt Borka's discarded beer from the shirt. Charlie couldn't resist saying to Emily, "That's what you call 'having a drink on me'." Emily frowned from not understanding Charlie's comment, and Charlie decided to stop making attempts at humour. There were no heartfelt goodbyes exchanged by anyone, except for Emily. She wished Charlie well with his house. Borka stormed off to his vehicle and Mr Kreatin told Charlie all the snag list was explained. Cunningly, before turning to walk away, he also reminded Charlie not to forget the money transfer and how the permissions could still be reversed.

He didn't want to go back into the hotel, as he'd been inside all day. Instead, he strolled to his house and would call Magdalena from upstairs while looking at the view. As he walked, he focused on the smell of the countryside and its uniqueness. Thinking how difficult it would be to manufacture its smell in bottle form, he wondered about its ingredients. There was the smell of fresh-cut trees, burning logs, clay ovens, food being cooked, herbs, flowers… maybe even goat droppings added to the aroma. Arriving at his house and climbing the stairs, he stepped onto a second balcony that day. Though this was his own one, providing a much more spectacular view. Taking phone in hand, he called Magdalena.

"Hello Charlie, how are you?" she enthusiastically asked on hearing his voice.

"Fine thanks, Magdalena, I heard from Emily you're still in Sofia. It'd be nice to see you again," he replied.

"Oh, so you know Emily. Of course, and it'll be good to see you again. I'll be back in Ovineshta soon. Charlie, I want to ask you something," she requested.

"Yes fine, what is it?" he replied.

"My father called me the other day. He told me he saw you with a woman on one of your balconies, is it true and who is she?" she asked in an accusing manner. Charlie was stunned for a moment by what she said, as it was completely unexpected. Also, he had to quickly recollect that time on the balcony with that woman. It was Vanya the masseur from Bonkas. Charlie offered to show her his house and the special view from a balcony. However, he had to contrive a story for Magdalena about Vanya. That, so not to create any further suspicion of something which was completely innocent. "Oh yes, that woman. She was an estate agent. I called her to come view and value the property," he replied.

"Aha, my father said he couldn't see any daylight between the two of you. Charlie is she more than just an estate agent to you?" she asked.

"Oh that, she's very short-sighted and had to stand close to see me and no, no more than an estate agent," he feebly replied.

Magdalena seemed not very convinced of his story and continued probing. "Mm, strange as it must be difficult for her to value a property's construction if her eyesight is as bad as that. Can she see anything smaller than a wall?"

Charlie hoped the sarcastic remark was a sign of Magdalena's attempt at humour and not a continuation of interrogation. "Ha, of course she can. What's fascinating is *your* father's eyesight. His house must be five hundred metres away and I'm stunned to hear he can see the goings-on, on my balcony that clearly?" he exclaimed.

"Ha, that's right. He has a pair of binoculars and that's why. There is a bit of a story about them," she replied.

"I see, okay, I'm curious, you can tell me if you want," he said while feeling relieved to be deflecting her attention from Vanya.

"Okay, my father wanted to become a policeman, but didn't because my parents left him their farm. So, his plans changed, but he still had a strong sense of law and order.

He would walk the streets of Ovineshta at night to make sure they were safe. That's when he met my mum. They passed each other one winter's evening, while she walked home. She worked the night shift at the laundry factory. It cleaned many hotels' bed linen. My father instantly liked her, and they would stop to chat over several nights. Knowing she cleaned bed linen, he cheekily suggested, if she showed him her bed linen, he would show her his own. Obviously, she refused and walked on, but liked his cheeky comment. They finally decided to date but she was living with her parents, making it difficult for him to visit her at home privately. After a long think, they came up with a plan. She would hang a certain coloured cloth on her clothesline, signalling it was okay for him to visit her. He bought a pair of binoculars so he could see her clothesline. That's why he has binoculars, Charlie," she explained.

"Ha that's a great story, Magdalena. Your parents are characters, for sure. Anyway, it'll be good to see you again when you're back home," he replied.

"Yes, me too, but I want to say we keep it friends for now, okay?" she asked.

"Of course, that's fine by me. The main thing from this is that you know nothing strange went on with Vanya, as you obviously thought," he explained.

"Fine, Charlie, I believe you and see you soon," she replied. Sensing the conversation was coming to an end and he was vindicated, he squeezed one more line into their chat. One he'd later regret. "Oh Magdalena, it would've been more suspicious if your father saw more women on the other balcony," he said, making a feeble laugh. Magdalena only responded with a goodbye.

They hung up and regardless of his last comment, his stomach felt hollow. Her request for them to stay as friends struck him a little hard, giving him a weakness. He wasn't completely convinced she no longer had suspicions about Vanya's visit. Still standing on the balcony, he looked down the valley to reflect over the conversation. He wondered if he would still be in Ovineshta for Magdalena's return, as he needed to fly back to London very soon.

His plane landed at Heathrow Airport with Charlie staring out at the runway. A feeling of regret occupied his mind at not seeing Magdalena before he left Ovineshta. He was convinced seeing her again would give him the chance to remove any residual thoughts about her mistrust. He missed her home arrival by just a day because a necessity requiring him to return to London. The loft was finished and he looked forward to seeing it. More so now because it would act as an antidote to his partially lost love. The finished loft also meant taking his final payment, which would be very welcome – seeing as he had to pay Mr Kreatin almost €10,000.

On approaching the house next morning, he saw a makeshift sign standing on the pavement and leaning against the garden wall. It read, 'Exorcisms by Orthodox Priest. Free your House of Evil. Starting from £200. Call Nikolov on…'

"Oh my god, it's retail exorcisms now with him and Nelly," Charlie exclaimed. He didn't go in but instead went across the road to monitor the house from a distance. He knew the loft was to be exorcised after its completion and didn't want to walk in during the ceremony. Still watching in secret from across the road, Nelly appeared with her fake priest after fifteen minutes. An exchange of money took place between her and Nikolov before he walked off and she went back inside. He waited for another while before going in to allow any post-ceremony chat to die down.

After entering, all seemed as he expected going by previous visits. He went straight upstairs to the loft. No one was there and on first sight it looked beautiful. Then he heard Nelly calling, "Charlie, is that you?"

"Hi Nelly, yes, come up," he replied.

"Charlie, you just missed the second exorcism," she said excitedly.

"Well, I guessed it was going on for two reasons. The advertising board outside and those things hanging from the ceiling must have something to do with it," he replied.

"Oh no! Nikolov forgot to take that sign with him. He thinks he can make a business from it. I must hide it," she said. Then, looking up, she informed Charlie, "Those up there, more stuff from the park to ward off evil spirits?"

He was only partly focused on Nelly's recalling of the exorcism because he had the final payment on his mind. The pleasing thought of money coming his way created a forgiving mood within. It resulted in a slightly more casual attitude to this second act of deceitfulness by Nelly and friend. Even so and despite his changed mood, he thought it right to reprimanded her and said, "Nelly, you've been out of order with all your trickery and any original fun from the first time is well and truly forgotten now. Then about that sign outside, is he mad? He won't stop at anything now seeing he's gone this far. Maybe you'll hear of him offering to exorcise two houses for the price of one."

Nelly looked like a chastised girl but protested, "Come on, Charlie, I know it's naughty but if it makes her feel good, why not? How many people are taking useless tablets thinking they help them when they don't? Those companies which make them are a lot worse than this silly game."

Charlie relented and didn't admonish her any further. "Okay, whatever. Anyway, it's done now. Actually, where is Ms Belcher? I haven't heard her yet. Out of interest, I wonder what type of flowers are hanging up there?" he asked.

Nelly restored her mischievous grin and said, "I don't know but the smell doesn't match their appearance. They smell weird and maybe of foxes or dog pee," she said while stifling a laugh.

"Phew, yes. What about Ms Belcher?" he asked.

"She didn't want to be here for this loft exorcism, and I think she went back to where she was born. A village in Derbyshire, I think. Dick knows more, but she's even more mental now, Charlie, and her journey back home is for weird reason I think, like witchcraft or something. She knows bitchcraft already so witchcraft should be easy for her to learn. There's only one letter difference," she replied with a laugh. Charlie couldn't resist laughing, too, and Nelly quickly took advantage of his lightened mood by saying, "You know, my friend looked up song lyrics to use for the exorcism. He chose Cliff Richard's 'Devil Woman' and chanted the words in Bulgarian again. Good choice, you think, Charlie?"

Charlie narrowed his eyes and gave a scornful look as he turned away, saying, "Tch, bad Nelly. I must go downstairs and see Dick for some money."

"Oh," said Nelly and continuing to hold Charlie's attention, "She plans to do a long holiday in America when back from Derbyshire." Charlie turned to only look.

Nelly then half turned away from him before delivering her final 'flick of the tail' at Ms Belcher. She said, "You know how they have a 'Rust Belt' and a 'Bible Belt' in America? Well, they'll have a 'Bitch Belt' if she decides to do that holiday." The delay dissuaded Charlie from commenting, though he found himself smiling as he descended the stairs two steps at a time.

As he came off the last stair tread onto the ground floor hall, he saw a woman through the glass of the front door. "Ah, she's back from Derbyshire," he mumbled as he approached the door.

Swinging it back slowly, he saw a stranger looking at him and say, "Hello, are you the man doing exorcisms?"

Charlie denied knowing anything about it, made excuses for the sign and removed it after the woman left.

Next, he went to Dick for his money and talked about the finished loft with him. "Charlie, we must have paid you too much for the job. I was looking around the loft and sizing up the storage space behind the new partition. There was a half-eaten sourdough and foie gras sandwich left on a joist," he said enthusiastically.

Charlie was as confused about its reason for being there, as he knew nothing of Tagaby's secret overnight stays. Dick wore the look of a detective who'd just disclosed important information on a case. while not knowing what the case was about. The two went up to the loft to have a look together and talk over its merits. While climbing the stairs, Dick stated that the exorcism was poppycock, and in a manner suggesting he had superior knowledge and judgement. Nelly popped into the loft to join them, and her comments added to the positivity of the new work. All three felt synced in perfect harmony for that moment. Though it was abruptly ended by Dick's sudden outburst from a sudden realisation.

"Oh no, the sandwich!" he exclaimed.

"What, what is it?" a perplexed Charlie asked.

"The foie gras and sourdough are what was taken from the fridge on the night of the supposed ghost visit. It's the same food as in the loft. It's proof that whatever it was, has been up here too," he announced and paired it with a confused look at his own statement. He continued, "Phew, good job we have it exorcised."

"You've suddenly changed your tune. A minute ago, you called it poppycock," said Charlie. They all left the loft, Dick looking flushed and feeling weaker while descending the stairs. The combination of a sudden realisation of a potential truth he had earlier dismissed, plus, acting fickle-minded had embarrassed him.

Back on the ground floor and standing together in the hall, Charlie told Nelly he'd pop by again and see her. Dick, trying to reclaim credibility and reassert his authority, said, "Yes you will because you still haven't fixed the toilet catch my wife requested."

"Ah, sorry, of course. How did I keep forgetting that?" Charlie replied apologetically and continued, "Okay, I'll come round tomorrow." He left for home and while on his way, decided to call Mr Kreatin after settling down indoors.

"Hello Charlie, how wonderful to hear your voice," he said on taking Charlie's call. It was the thought of Charlie transferring the rest of the €10,000 which really made him feel wonderful. "Thank you, Mr Kreatin, I'll transfer the money tomorrow. I'm wondering about my house, is Borka back working on it?" he enquired. Mr Kreatin promised Charlie he would call Borka every two days to make sure he was on the job. Charlie planned to send only €5.000 the next morning and maybe even delay it together with the outstanding for as long as he dared. It would help encourage Mr Kreatin to honour his word about supervising Borka.

The next morning, Charlie visited Dick as promised, to fix the toilet door lock. There was a strong smell of air freshener in the closet, a probable sign of Nelly having had a secret cigarette. While fixing the lock, he thought of Dick's newfound superstition. He imagined him in his civil service office and laying tarot cards on his leather inlaid desk to guide him in decision making. Or, maybe searching for guidance by reading tea leaves in the bottom of a government canteen teacup. Charlie went to the kitchen to look for him. "Mr Fruit, are you there? I've fixed the lock," he said. "Hi, come in. Okay, good. I suppose you're off now," he replied.

"Yes, how's Ms Belcher? Nelly said she's gone to Derbyshire," he asked.

"Oh yes, basically she's into revisiting her past to try deal with her madness. There's her new penchant for learning witchcraft too. I don't know where her delving will stop," he said.

Charlie sensed a previously unseen edginess from Dick and decided to play on it. "I see, yes, it's a concern and more so if she really embraces witchcraft. She could put a spell on you. A bit like Prince Charming being turned into a frog for unfaithfulness to his future wife," he stated.

Dick looked at him with an expressionless face but reciprocated Charlie's ridicule. "Mm, yes, in my case, it'd be because of the booze and not women. She'd probably turn me into a duck instead of a frog. I'd have to go to an off-licence or pub and ask the manager to kiss me human again," he replied. Then quickly adding, he said, "Anyway, we'll see. I'm a bit busy now, so you can let yourself out." Those final few dismissive words were to remind Charlie of his place and who was ultimately in charge of the domain. Charlie knew it too. He went upstairs one more time to say goodbye to Nelly and for them to keep in touch. Then, he left for home.

He decided to make two important calls the next morning. One to Mr Kreatin and the other to Evelina. Knowing when the work and corrections were to be completed would help him choose the earliest flight for an inspection. Furniture still had to be bought, too. Bulgaria was ahead in time by two hours, and he called Kreatin in the early part of the morning. He knew it was better to have fresh and focused minds when discussing business.

"Hello Mr Kreatin, this is Charlie," he said.

"Hello Charlie, I can't see that money in my account. You have more money for me?" he asked.

"Ah no, sorry, Mr Kreatin, please give a bit more time as I'm waiting for some money from my work," he replied.

"Okay, I can't stay long as have a busy day. What do you want?" he asked with a slightly agitated voice.

"It's about Borka and progress with the works list. I want to fly over again to inspect as soon as possible, and I have furniture to buy," he enquired. Before Mr Kreatin could reply, Charlie quickly added, "Oh, I could bring some cash to you, too." He knew that last comment would be a sweetener for him and provide Charlie with as favourable a reply as he could possibly expect.

Mr Kreatin's mock affable manner returned on hearing the mention of money and he replied, "Ah, wonderful and thank you. Well, have no fear my good Charlie, I'm on his back and he tells me he'll finish everything in ten days."

"Thanks Mr Kreatin, I'll let you go now. See you soon," he said. Next call to make was to Evelina and fortunately for him, she was available too. The curtains were ready, and Charlie told her she could plan a visit from ten days' time to fit them. He was relieved to have those calls done and made a cup of tea before booking another flight.

Chapter 10

He touched down twelve days after his chat with Mr Kreatin, instead of the originally planned ten days. The two-day delay was of no matter to Charlie and might have been useful for Borka, in case of any hold-ups with work. Even if it still wasn't finished, he knew it would be very close, with only minor cosmetic works remaining. Passing through the airport he grabbed a leaflet advertising an art exhibition in Sofia. After closer reading he saw it was an abstract expressionism exhibition by post world two war painters such as Jackson Pollock. He made a mental note to visit it before his return to London. Another two-and-three-quarter hours he was in Bonkas strolling around the town. He didn't want to go straight to Ovineshta and his house, but rather stopped off in Bonkas. The reason being to enjoy and savour the anticipation of what he was about to see. People often rush through their anticipations of positive experiences to come. Charlie thought they should be enjoyed and prolonged it for as much as he liked. He knew the next view of his house would be his final surprise sight. Afterwards, there'd be no more changes, no more anticipation of what he'd see. Every future visit to the house would provide the same expectant view. He remembered the first trip and the elation from his anticipation of finding his plot. Then, in contrast, his apprehension of that meeting with Borka and Mr Kreatin. The other experiences during all his trips passed through his mind like fractals, they whizzed by his mind's eye until they became just a blur. After feeling satisfied with this indulgence, he switched focus onto finding a taxi to finally visit his – hopefully - finished house.

"Hello driver, Ovineshta, please?" asked Charlie.

"No problem, sir," replied the driver. A few seconds after getting into the car, the driver said, "I recognise you from somewhere, some paper or something. Maybe you famous."

Charlie immediately thought of the police posters and changed the subject. "Ha, I see, no I'm an ordinary man living an ordinary life. I picked up a leaflet in Sofia airport about an exhibition and must visit it when I return. It's about abstract painters, interesting. You like art?" He kept talking to distract the driver from trying to recall where he saw his face. "After the war, some painters experimented with new methods for applying paint, like spilling and throwing it onto canvases for different effects."

The driver suddenly turned his head sideways, signalling something of interest was just spoken by Charlie. The driver said, "My partner hurt back from throwing paint."

"Ah, interesting. Is she successful, famous maybe?" asked Charlie.

"No, not successful but she could be famous very soon if she carries on – famous among the police especially," he replied with a laugh.

Charlie was confused by his response. He thought, "Not being successful, yet very soon to be famous was a contradiction in terms surely."

"I see, how does she throw? Is it on a floor canvas?" asked Charlie with increasing curiosity.

"No, walls," he replied.

"Oh okay, I can see how throwing paint upwards, and a distance could cause back problems," suggested Charlie.

"Yes, and five litre tins are heavy. After throwing so many she has a pulled muscle," he replied.

Charlie's face suddenly dropped and froze. He sat back in his seat and listened to his heart quicken. A hot flush completed the chain of sensations form his realisation. A realisation that the driver's partner was the estranged wife of the man building the hotel in Ovineshta. He felt a fool for not realising earlier in the conversation. He chose not to tell the driver he knew about the story and said, "Okay, I've built a house in Ovineshta and am visiting it now."

"Now I definitely know you because I know about that house and the foreigner. I'm happy for you, it's a lovely town. If you need cheap paint, I can get some for you – but it's black," he said. Charlie decided not to tell the driver he knew about the scandal of the woman. Though, he nearly accidentally revealed his knowledge of it, by asking why she chose black paint to throw over the hotel walls. Both reached their destination with the driver remaining oblivious to Charlie knowing the whole story. He got out of the taxi at Hotel Rumyana for another stay.

"Hello again, Charlie, your house has been busy with workmen," said Rumyana on seeing him walk through the hotel entrance.

"Hello Rumyana, hope you're well. That's great to hear. I'm particularly keen to see it this time and hopefully finished too. You and Petar can come around to visit the day after next. I'll ask a few more people to call by, too," he replied. He went upstairs to relax a while before going back down to eat. While looking up at the ceiling, he planned the next couple of days. Evelina would be arriving lunchtime tomorrow with the curtains, so he decided to go to his house early. It would allow him plenty of time to inspect Borka's finished works and do any necessary cleaning. He planned to call Magdalena tomorrow and invite her for a look at the now completed house. Then finally, he'd call Vanya offering her another visit. Refreshed and ready for his meal, Charlie went down to the restaurant. After ordering, he decided not to delay the calls and made them while his meal was cooking. Both Magdalena and Vanya answered and both were keen to visit again. He wasn't sure if Vanya fully understood his – slightly improved – Bulgarian but hoped she did and would appear. Happy with his plans for the next couple days, he looked forward to bed, but not before his phone rang. It was Mr Kreatin calling from Sofia to ask about the outstanding money. Charlie, sensing his irritation and urgency to receive it, said he'd go to Sofia in three days to pay him.

The weather was as reliable as ever that summer and Charlie woke to another sunny day. His mind felt particularly free of clutter that very moment. Maybe it was because the loft in London was now finished along with his Bulgarian house which gave him that sense. The vacuum enticed him to fill it with some other thoughts and it was his future which won his attention. He imagined living in Bulgaria with Magdalena for his wife. Though he left that idyll thought after reminding himself of her aborting any deeper involvement with him. "Mm, shame. What to do with myself," he muttered. His stomach rumbled for food, taking his mind back to the present time. He went downstairs to enjoy a full breakfast before setting off for his house.

As it came into view, he immediately spotted the new corner stonework. "Ah, great, hopefully everything else is done," he thought. On approaching it, he walked around the outside for an inspection. He remained pleased, as all the outside was painted. Then, standing back from the house a little and holding a hand to shade his eyes, he spied the problem post. Despite straining his eyes to see better, he couldn't detect if the split post had been replaced. Next was the inside. His apprehension about what he might see made him decide on a preview first. He slowly approached a window and peered through it, unsure of what he'd see. The pane of glass was dirty and prevented him from recognising anything inside clearly. The delay and inability to see properly made him fret a little and he walked quickly to open the door. He hoped the next sight after entering would dispel any reason for his apprehension. Slowly stepping inside and walking straight to the kitchen, he saw it was completed. Breathing a sigh of relief, he relaxed and turned around to see all the walls decorated.

Just as tensions relaxed, he said, "Crikey, hang on, I forgot the water." He moved quickly to the sink to check with one hand, while crossing two fingers of the other. He watched the water pour out of the tap making him automatically think of the other service - electricity. Still holding crossed fingers, he switched on a light, anticipating a glow from the ceiling. No light came on but – after a closer look – he saw the only problem was a missing lightbulb. He strolled around the ground floor for another few seconds to enjoy his expectations realised before going upstairs.

The split post was on his mind as he climbed the stairs. He walked the landing to both bathrooms and saw renewed toilet suites and secure tiling. "Fine, that's great, phew, now and finally the post," he said out loud. Standing at the doorway to that balcony, he stared at the post. He wanted to believe it was renewed before moving closer to inspect properly for a replacement.

It wasn't! Borka had filled the split and Charlie was convinced it had warped and twisted slightly more since his last visit. It wasn't enough for most people to notice, but his tradesman eyes saw such fine irregularities. "Okay, don't let it bother you now, one neglected snag out of many more corrected is all right for now. Even though that post is important because it's structural, I'll leave it for now," he told himself while staring at it. Evelina was arriving in a few hours with curtains, and he had a house to clean.

He went to the hardware shop on the corner of the square for cleaning items. While walking, he remembered the argument which had taken place outside the shop that day. One person was already inside when he arrived and a second came in after him. Looking around the shelves for cleaning stuff allowed him to look at those in the shop. Charlie was certain the second customer was the man building the hotel. After moving closer, he was able to study him better. He had a focused, business look but also seemed harmless and non-threatening in manner and appearance. Charlie planned to delay outside after leaving to hopefully have a chance to talk with him. In a while, both met face to face and looked at each other. Charlie saluted, followed by a mention of the weather. He hoped his accent would create enough curiosity to provoke a response from the man. It did.

"Hello, you're not from here, are you?" asked the man.

"No, I'm from London, England and I built a house here," said Charlie.

"Neither am I, I'm from Ruse. Like you, I'm building, but a hotel. It's not too big, though," he replied.

The man was middle-aged, wearing working clothes and seemed polite. Understating his hotel was a sign he didn't carry an inflated ego, which often accompanied businessmen. They were both happy to continue chatting in the warm sun. "My name is Stoyan. I had a lot of trouble with her in there, you know," he said while throwing a sideways look at the shop. He continued to explain about the disruption to his marriage over his wife's misunderstanding about him and his landlady. Charlie acted ignorant to the whole tale but remained attentive. He was curious to hear his side of the story and of any developments with the saga.

There was and Stoyan said, "I had to get a guard dog to deter her from constantly damaging the new work. Unfortunately, the dog was lazy and wouldn't bark at anything. So, I bought some perfume which I know my wife uses and sprinkled it all over a coat. I wore the coat and walked around my guard dog, so it'd get used to the smell. After a few times of that, I then kicked the dog in the backside to make it hostile to the smell," he explained.

Charlie was smiling and said, "So what happened"

"I had the dog chained so I knew it couldn't run too far to catch me if it attacked. It did. I slipped and fell after I ran away and it bit my back. So, I have a painful back now for my trouble. I just hope when my back heals, my dog still guards. Otherwise, it's all been a waste of time."

As he told the story, Charlie laughed within and liked him more and more. His appeal came from telling his story with a masculine regret, rather than any extreme animosity towards his wife. Charlie felt the need to offer something in return by way of reciprocating the man after exposing his soul. "Stoyan, I really regret your plight, but you may be surprised to hear the following. I know about your plight and have positive news for you," said Charlie.

"Oh, you really surprise me. What is that?" he asked with quizzical eyes and half a smile.

"Your wife's new partner drove me from Bonkas yesterday and she popped up in the conversation. She has a bad back too, from throwing all those five litre tins of paint at your hotel. It seems she's in bed nursing it. I got the impression from him that she will stop throwing it now," said Charlie while hoping for an enthusiastic response.

"Ah, so we both have bad backs from this problem. Isn't it a coincidence? It makes me think are there heavenly forces at work in our dispute? A relief, though, and yes, hopefully she'll stop. Well, I must go now and nice speaking with you," he replied.

Charlie's final words were, "I'm showing my house to a few local friends tomorrow, will you come along for a glass of wine and chat around one pm?"

"Thank you, I will," he replied. Charlie stayed with him for the short walk before the forked roads took them their separate ways. Charlie cleaned for the rest of the morning and welcomed a tired Evelina in the afternoon. The two talked and hung curtains in the clean and fresh-smelling house. Evelina drove back to Sofia and Charlie strolled back to Hotel Rumyana for a meal and sleep.

It was his last day in Ovineshta, even though he wanted to stay longer. He envisaged a friendly, happy day of bonding between some local people in his house. Hopefully everyone would have a glass or two of wine while chatting. Rumyana offered him some light folding chairs to use temporarily for the gathering. Charlie walked up to the house with them over two trips. They were light so he didn't mind carrying them on foot. Afterwards he bought a few bottles of wine and left them in his brand-new kitchen. Two workmen were on the dirt road outside his house, surveying it prior to tarmacking. They looked downwards at the road and talked to each other while occasionally kicking a stone. A new tarmac road was a bonus for the house as it would add to its attraction. He stood and watched them from inside for a while. They turned their attention to a tree on the side of the road. He wondered if they would be removing it. Two of its branches stretched out across the road at about two and a half meters high. The men looked along the branches a few times to consider whether they were a concern for vehicles.

Turning his attention back to preparations, Charlie suddenly exclaimed, "Ah, no tea towel. Can't do without that when washing glasses." He strolled down to the square at his ease and searched for a suitable shop while thinking of anything else he might have forgotten.

Returning to his house and seeing it from a distance, he saw Magdalena and someone else standing by the door. He quickened his pace and eventually saw her friend was Emily. "Sorry, Magdalena and Emily, I didn't notice the time going by. I had to go buy a tea towel," he said apologetically.

Magdalena was in her provocative mood and said, "Charlie, leaving one woman waiting is bad but two is very, very neglectful. I hope you have something stronger than tea inside too." All laughed and went inside. Despite the laugh, Charlie was pleased, but also surprised at her flirty mood. Previously, she had made clear their relationship was to be a platonic one. So, Charlie reasoned that it allowed her to tempt and tease him without fear of it being taken as an invite for further advances from him! Whatever the reason for her behaviour, Charlie didn't deliberate any longer and focused on enjoying the get-together. Vanya turned up a while later and so too did Petar and Stoyan. After initial introductions were made among those who were strangers, a group formed on both floors, The women went to an upstairs balcony and the men stayed downstairs. Charlie enjoyed listening to the strange new sounds of chatter in his house from the kitchen. He stood motionless for a while to focus on its sound. There was something nice about listening to friendly conversation despite not hearing what was spoken. It made the house feel lived in and homely.

Feeling contented, he looked back down at a bottle of wine he was about to open. Just as he offered corkscrew to cork, all the harmony up until then was suddenly interrupted! A scream came from upstairs at the same time as a sound of snapping timber! Charlie instantly shouted, "Oh no, the dodgy post!"

Running out of the kitchen and past a surprised Petar and Stoyan, he raced upstairs. He ran through the bedroom and stopped suddenly at the balcony door. All was fine and the women looked with bemusement at Charlie, wondering what was wrong! "What is it Charlie, what's wrong?" asked Magdalena.

"Phew, sorry, I thought something happened when I heard you scream," he gasped, followed by a relieved smile. Still wanting to know what made the loud sound of snapping timber, he turned to look out of a window on the other side of the room. He saw the two workmen swinging off a branch of the roadside tree. Another branch was lying on the road. Relieved at knowing the reason for the sound, he turned back round to face the women and asked, "Oh by the way, why were you screaming or shrieking?"

The fun atmosphere resumed after he asked the question and Magdalena replied, "Vanya was telling me about the mistake in the apartment over the massage in front of the estate agent – ha." A relaxed Charlie joined in the laugh, then went downstairs to finish opening the new bottle of wine.

Stoyan and Petar made a good friendship match as they were businessmen with hotels. Charlie refilled their glasses before going back upstairs to do the same for the women. Just as he approached the first step of the stairs, his phone rang. Returning to the kitchen to take the call in privacy, he wondered who it could be. Looking down at his screen, he saw it was Dick from London. "Hello Dick, surprised to hear from you, are you all right?" he asked.

"Yes, as well as can be I suppose. I'm just calling to ask if you can pop around to rehang the mirrors. Some are quite heavy and I can't manage," he asked.

"Oh, not a problem Dick. In a few days, if that's okay? How's Sue?" he asked. A silence followed and was almost long enough to prompt Charlie to repeat the question.

Finally, Dick spoke. "Oh, I don't care about what I say any more and whoever finds out about her dysfunctionality. She's really done it this time. My name is mud and hers too," he snapped.

"Oh, what happened?" enquired Charlie.

"You know that visit back to her childhood in Derbyshire? She just got pissed all the time in the village and ended up getting arrested," he said.

"Well, that's not as bad as what I could have heard," he replied, and in a way to soften the upset for Dick.

"It is bad because she wasn't just arrested for being drunk and disorderly, she was naked in a public place, too. She was leaning against a post and rail fence on a roadside bend with no clothes on one evening. God knows how many car drivers saw her rear end in their headlights. My brother-in-law called to tell me the news. The call took ages because he was laughing so much. She met some childhood boyfriend by the name of Stellon or Stallon or some similar name one night. They got drunk before re-enacting a photo they took when young. There was a tailback of traffic while this went on because he was also drunk and staggering around the road trying to take her picture. I don't know, disaster. Every motorist in the county must've seen her. A disaster," he exclaimed. Charlie remembered Nelly telling him about the old photos she found of Sue in a drawer.

Dick continued, "I'm told the picture is going around the village. I thought I might as well ask for a copy as I haven't seen her arse in decades. Not that it's anything to talk about as she never had a great figure. I can't help thinking the motorists must have thought they were in one of those scary ghost train rides when her rear came into view. My brother-in-law laughed because he thought I was joking about requesting a picture and not seeing her rear in years. I wasn't but I didn't tell him it was the truth. To be honest, I enjoyed someone laughing at what they thought was a joke made by myself. No one ever has previously."

Charlie offered sympathies while unable to stop his muted laughter. Dick didn't want to delay much longer after realising all the personal scandal he had divulged. He said he would see Charlie in a few days and finished the call by asking one more thing. It was to be a further surprise for Charlie.

"Charlie, that Bulgarian priest who came here, I decided to go visit his church and used the post code he gave me. It's not for a church, but Horse Guards' Parade! Do you know anything about it?" he exclaimed.

Charlie took the phone from his ear and winced as he looked out of the kitchen window. He paused to wonder how he should reply, while the women upstairs still waited for more wine. Deciding to play ignorant, he said, "No Dick, not a clue." After a few more minutes of chat, they hung up. Charlie remained stationary and only allowed himself a few seconds to dwell on the conversation. Then, left the kitchen in haste with a newly opened bottle of wine for the patient women upstairs. Stoyan asked if everything was all right.

Stopping with one foot on the bottom step of the stairs, Charlie turned and said with a slightly concentrated look, "Yes, fine. That was just someone I know in London looking for a church which doesn't exist… housing a priest who is really a guitarist in a rock band… and how his – the caller's – wife was arrested for being drunk and naked in public. Let me top up the women's glasses and I'll be back," replied Charlie.

Stoyan and Petar gave each other very confused looks with Stoyan saying in perfect English, "And I thought my wife was mad!"